Cookie

A Fort Worth Story

Delphine Publications, LLC

9439 Everton Ct.

San Antonio, TX 78245

ISBN-13: 978-0-9821455-3-1

First printing July 2011

Printed in the United States

Edited by: Alanna Boutin

Cover Design: Odd Balls Designs

Layout: Write On Promotions

www.delphinepublications.com

www.tamikanewhouse.com

Dedicated to Daijah, you are my first, you are me, and I am you. Mama loves you

Acknowledgements

I sat down to write this book two years ago. This was the longest projetct ever and I think I know why. For those who don't know; this story is based on truth and I for one was afriad of how to tamper with that truth. I feel that though in the end I got it. This story was for my mother. I miss her so much because not only was she a mother, she was my best friend. Her character in here is strong and important because I want people to understand who she was to me and as a whole. Now I know throughout my career people will ask me, am I Cookie. I guess you need to read the book to find out huh?

I want to personally thank people who have helped me progress in my career till this point like Ni'Cola Mitchell. The only person of the same sex who I will lay down and die for. I also want to shout out my support system Marckus, Kayla, Sis Lo, and most of all Jr and Daijah. I love my children more than ever because I see me in them. I see my eyes, my mouth, my smile, my personality. They are a direct reflection of me and I love you two with all my heart.

Thank you to the book clubs who have supported me and the independent stores who have pushed my books. I want to shout out Devine of Books in the Hood, DC Book Diva, Laquita of Literary Joint, Tra in Baltimore, the street hustlers in Philly, and I can't forget my love for New York. Thank you Anika for proving poerty and writing "Cookie's Fortune". To my Delphine Publications family Anna, Jhamika, Felisha, Dee, and Norris thank you for trusting me to lead you. I hope I am doing my best.

With that said, sit back relax and enjoy the story of Latoya James and hint her name means something in real life. See if you can get it. ☺

Muah,

Tamika L. Newhouse

A Fort Worth Story

Cookies Fortune

One piece of paper changed my life

Eyes and finger numb as tears roll

narrow slits and low lids

my unlucky number are:

them making me feel less than 0

Type 2 diabetes

life dealing me crazy 8's

Pregnant before legal age :21

I'm broken and broke

I didn't think it would carry out this way

I have to stay in my mother's corner

Tell her that I'm fortunate to have her

Wipe the egg of my face every time someone drops my name

Seems like I'm cracking under pressure 24/7

Am I the only 1 feeling my heart crumble?

These 2 eyes have seen enough

I want just a piece of happiness, but I'll settle for my mothers

strength, courage and wisdom- a triple delight when I'm down

I want my life to unfold into good luck and happy endings

pick up the pieces to create order

Awaiting my special delivery

· searching for answers

I'm looking for fortune

Prologue

I remember those days when it was nothing but just us girls. Hanging, partying, thinking about life after high school. All those things a girl dreams about when she gets grown. That's a time I couldn't wait to come, my adulthood. As everyone used to say, I can do whatever I want to do when I get grown. Coming home when you wanted to, having sex without feeling guilty, having my own car, my own apartment. What fools we were. I honestly loved living in the house in the middle of the circle on our street and where all the neighbors were white and knew us from diapers. I miss the times when boys used to come knocking on Mama's door asking for me or Lyric to come out and play. I laugh at the word *play* 'cause that's what we did. Played nookie.

Mama was a large woman. She was a Bible-gripping, churchgoing, single mother with a tongue that could curse you out till next year, and a fist that could knock you into the next decade. No matter what I did, I made sure I got good grades, obeyed what she said, and never spoke about what I really was doing. A single mother can only do so much, and my mother did it all. She was the type to yell, "Do it, God," so loud your eardrums vibrated and your hair on the back of your neck stood up. She also was the one who punched you in the chest and whooped your ass when she caught a boy in your room.

Lyric and I were her only children, and like day and night, we didn't mix. She was the loud, outgoing type with the big breasts. I was the dark, slender, quiet type with a dull life. Hell, it wasn't until Lyric let me go out with her, when she used Mama's big white van, that I started to come out of my shell.

Come out of my shell——humph! I laugh at that because coming out is just what I did. The boys started to bark at my hips when they started to resemble Nia Long's, and I answered. They also loved my dark skin that tended to glow in the dark. I wasn't always so dark. A sista was bright, and then brown, and now just black as hell. Got it from Mama.

Mama stood at 5'11, 350 pounds, and had long locks. She wore a **Jheri** curl for at least twenty-five years now, and it only looked good on her. It wasn't the greasy curl everybody remembers. It looked more like hair a person would have if they were mixed with white and black. That kind folks called good hair. I wasn't too bad off myself. My hair trailed all the way down my back to my bra strap. I never needed to wear extensions.

I was tall, slender, dark, pretty, with long, black hair and a mouth that could go off like a fire engine. I guess I should have introduced myself at the beginning of this tale, huh? My name is Latoya James, but you can call me Cookie.

If Only He Knew

I followed my sister to the house party everyone was talking about. Yeah, I was young, but Mama never minded where I went when I was with Lyric. She was my older sister. She *should* have worried because this is when I had the most fun. Who else would be allowed to come home at three in the morning at the age of fourteen? This night was no different from some of the other nights when we went out. None of us were old enough to go to the club, so we always went to someone's party they were throwing at their house. Until just recently I was a homebody, not really worried about going out or meeting boys. That was until I entered Hills High School. They call us *fresh meat* when we first walked in the school doors. The seniors were lined up to get some freshman girl to fall in love with them, so that they can have sex with them whenever they wanted. Unfortunately for them, I wasn't that kind of girl.

I never got into my looks until I entered high school, and even then, I wasn't interested in every guy who walked my way. But I learned a lot from watching my sister, Lyric. She made many bad decisions in high school, and I wasn't about to follow suit. But when I got the opportunity to go out, I did.

Lyric's friend was throwing a house party. She was nineteen. Her older brother had bought alcohol and beer so all the young guys were throwing those drinks down. I don't know why I decided to go because I rarely openly talked to guys. As soon as we walked in the door, Lyric went her separate way, leaving me alone to fish away the dogs. I could hear them whispering around me. They were admiring my young figure, firm breasts, and hips. Yes, I was *fly*, as they say. But I was also shy as hell. Upset that Lyric left me alone, I walked back to the patio door and decided to sit in one of the chairs out there just to sit back and watch the crowd. This scene was new to me. I had no idea how to gain a guy's number or even tell him that I wanted to give him my number.

"Hey, Cookie, why are you just sitting around? Girl, get up and find you some nookie," Lynn yelled out, finding me in the back sitting quietly. She was obviously drunk because she was yelling so loud over the music. I wasn't about to dance with any boy around here. None were my type anyhow. Lynn and Lyric liked the thug type. I, on the other hand, like clean-cut and well-dressed guys. Those types of boys were not here tonight.

"I'm all right, Lynn. Dang, you're loud. Go ask Lyric how long we're going to be here."

"Girl, please. Lyric and Johnny are together, and you know it's going to be a long night. Ugh, you are *so* boring."

Johnny was one of Lyric's boyfriends. Just another guy I had to be nice to, knowing he wouldn't be around too much longer anyhow.

"Well, Cookie, I'll talk to you later," she said, as her boyfriend pulled her inside to dance.

I waved her off as I started to get mad at myself for coming to this party. It wasn't beneficial to me. Mama always let Lyric use the white van on the weekends. We called it, the "big body white." So every weekend we piled our friends inside and went rollin'. Most weekends were fun, but tonight was not one of those times. That was, until Carlos spotted me. I didn't know he knew people here. We went to the same church and all. I've known him since elementary school. He definitely was a looker. I've always had a big crush on him. It was just two years ago I was letting him kiss me in the back of our church. Yeah, that was a big risk back then because everyone there knew one another. If we got into trouble, our parents would know before we would have a chance to redeem ourselves. Carlos was one of my biggest crushes for so long. It kind of took me a long time to get him out of my system; I guess you can say he never will be. There's something about your first that leaves a lasting impression on you.

I must admit I hated my first kiss. It was wet, and it felt weird to have someone else's lips on mine. Shoot, I was only twelve; what did I know? We lost touch for a long time after he and his family moved. Now seeing him here gave me that old schoolgirl crush feeling again. I was weak in the knees behind this boy. His skin was perfect; he had a great smile, nice personality, and never gave me attitude like most boys. I hadn't seen him in some months, and here he was walking my way. Lord, let me sit up straight and act cute. This seemed just like the time for your hair to mess up or for you to look unappealing to the guy you couldn't stop dreaming about. I crossed my legs to show off my hips, which were starting to look more like a full-grown woman's hips every day.

"I knew that was you when I looked this way," he smiled.

"Hey, Carlos, long time no see. What are you doing here?" I wanted to say where the hell you been, but I couldn't act like his groupie.

"I know, right? Dang, girl, it's good to see you. You know, Lynn and I still see each other around, and she told me about her party. I didn't know Mama let you out this late."

"She does when I'm with Lyric." Carlos was two years older than I, just started driving his own car, and the older he got, the more girls noticed and wanted him.

He looked at me with that lustful stare. "You sure is looking good tonight. Do you want to dance?"

Oh, shoot, I hate dancing in public, I thought. But who is to say when I would see Carlos again, so I told him yes. He reached out for my hand. Boy, did I feel like I was touching a celebrity's hand. I was all giddy inside, but I couldn't show that I was nervous. I wanted to seem like a woman to him, and not the twelve-year-old girl who didn't know anything about kissing. His hand felt perfect in mine. He laced his fingers in between mine, as it was his habit to hold my hand this way. I brushed past some older couples nearly sexing on the dance floor, which was Lynn's backyard.

"All right, this is a good spot," he said as he twirled me around like Cinderella and pulled me into his embrace. He smelled like Old Spice, and for the first time, I felt my vagina get stiff. I didn't know what this feeling was. I felt hot, and my vagina throbbed with excitement. I didn't want Carlos to sense this sexual feeling I was getting. Thank heavens the music sped up, and we started to dance faster. I didn't have a lot of rhythm, but I had some.

He went to stand behind me so that my butt was pressed up against his midsection. I pointed my butt out toward him in hopes he felt how much of a woman I had become. I was very fine for a fourteen-year-old. I had a cup size C breasts, firm, shapely hips, and a round butt to go with it. I wasn't the typical brown-skinned girl. I embraced my dark skin. I loved it, and all the boys who lusted after me did as well. Carlos put his hands on my waist to help my butt stay in

4

place. I could tell he enjoyed my motions. I was enjoying the new rhythms I had just discovered. I got so lost in the dance, that I didn't realize how long we were dancing.

"Whew, I'm tired. Let's go grab a drink," I suggested.

"Yeah, me too. Let me go get us something." He ran off into the crowd. I went back to my chair I was sitting in before. I felt more confident this time walking back through the crowd.

"Oh, I see you have hooked up with Carlos. Girl, I thought you were over him." Lynn walked up to me wrapping her arm around my neck, whispering in my ear.

"Why didn't you tell me he was going to be here tonight?"

"I didn't know you and Carlos were still cool like that. I mean, it's been awhile. So what, y'all back together?"

"Naw, I mean I don't know. It depends."

"Okay, whatever, girl. Have fun. I'm going to go find your sister. She and Johnny together are bad for business."

"Oh, hey, Lynn," Carlos yelled out, giving her a hug as she passed by. They whispered something to each other, and I knew it was about me. Because I was the youngest, Lynn and Lyric tended to stay in my business. Out of the corner of my eye I saw Lyric's other friend Kyra walk outside yelling Lynn's name. Carlos walked back over to me and handed me a Sprite.

"Thanks," I said, grabbing the drink. "Were you and Lynn talking about me?"

He laughed a little and said, "Guilty. She just told me to be careful, that's all. I know how she and Lyric are."

"Yeah, I know." I took a sip of my drink.

5

"I'm sorry for not keeping in touch, you know. I mean, with the move and new school, it was hard keeping up with old friends."

"Old friends, huh?"

"Well, you know, I mean, friends for a long time. I know we were more than friends. I'm just saying sorry I didn't keep in touch. You know, when I saw you I got that old feeling again."

"The one you used to tell me about?"

"Yeah, you got some kind of spell on me, girl," he said, as he gently pushed my knee. I smiled from ear to ear. He used to tell me how he got anxious and nervous at the sight of me. How he couldn't wait to just get one hug from me. Hugging was all we could do without our families getting suspicious of our crushes.

"I must admit, I didn't think I would see you again. There was no good-bye. No I'll see you one day. Nothing." I tried not to sound hurt, but he was my first kiss. I couldn't help but to be hurt. I knew I was his past. He was a junior in high school now, almost an adult. He didn't have time for young girls like me. He got up to sit closer to me on the patio cement next to my chair. He looked up into my eyes. I hadn't been kissed since him, and I felt this night was going to be another one of those moments.

"I'm sorry, Cookie. I mean, what could I do? My parents had just gotten a divorce; I didn't have a car. I didn't know what to do. I didn't forget about you. How could I? We used to be like this growing up." He held up his two fingers and crossed them around each other. He knew what to say and when to say it. He used to stutter when he talked to me, mainly because he was nervous. But I could tell he was different now. He had a taste of freedom, and he was no longer afraid to speak to girls.

6

"I guess that is true. I had to get used to not seeing you. Not having you around. It was different, but I got over it," I said.

He looked confused. I didn't mean to sound like I was mad at him and was now over him because I wasn't. "What does that mean?" he asked.

"I'm sorry. Just speaking out of anger. I know you were limited on how you could see me. Shoot, look at me. I'm only fourteen. I wish I was older," I whispered.

"I got a car now. Did Lynn tell you that?"

"Yeah, I heard."

"Well ...?"

"Well, what?"

"You think Mama will let me come and see you?"

I got excited for a minute. "You want to come and see me?"

"Yes."

"You know Mama loves you. Shoot, when your parents didn't want us to communicate, she allowed you to call the house. I don't see why not."

He stared at me for a long time. I allowed him to stare, wondering what he was seeing in me. I finally asked, "What are you looking at?"

"I'm sorry for staring. It's just that you grew up. I mean, look at you. You look like a grown woman."

"You grew up yourself. You're not chubby anymore," I said, squeezing his cheeks. "I see you trying to get some muscles."

"Aw, come on, don't be teasing me now. Life has gotten better since we moved, though. And you—man, don't let me get started."

"What?" I laughed.

7

"How you move. Who taught you how to dance like that, Lyric?"

"Oh, so I was good, huh?" I boasted.

"Hell, yeah. I liked it a lot. I couldn't believe I was dancing with you," he said, placing his hand on my thigh.

"It's so good seeing you, Carlos. You have no idea how much I just wished you would have called me."

He leaned up and kissed me on my cheek. "I got a little wild when we moved. You know, I felt I was just let out of jail. I took my new freedom and ran with it. Time passed by, and I felt like I shouldn't call, like you would hate me. I didn't know what you would say to me when I walked over tonight. But I had to try. I couldn't risk running away and having you see me turn my back on you. You wouldn't have understood my motives."

I took a deep sigh, forcing back the tears that were coming to my eyes. I didn't want to believe Carlos was my first love. He was just a great friend of mine of the opposite sex. We shared passionate kisses, passionate hugs, and felt like we were two souls driven away because of our age. Having to hear this from him made me emotional.

He took my hand and said, "Let me show you my new car."

I usually didn't follow boys like that, but Carlos was family. If there was a boy I would trust to be alone with, he would be it. We walked around to the front of Lynn's house, and I noticed his new Monte Carlo. Seemed like every guy had to have this car or a Caprice.

"Oh, Carlos, this is nice, and it's clean," I laughed.

"Yeah, it's clean. This is my new baby." I teased him with a puffed lip and pretended to be jealous. "Oh, besides you, that is. Go on and sit in the driver's seat."

8

I kicked off my sandals and allowed my toes to touch the cold metal as I sat in the driver's seat.

"So I'll ask Mama about you coming over. Maybe she'll cook something I know you used to love, like her beans and corn bread."

He sat back in his passenger seat and seemed at peace. More relaxed than before. "Yeah, that's cool. Here, let me get your number." He pulled out his cell phone and typed in my number. "Do you hang out with Lyric and Lynn like this a lot?"

"I just started. It's cool. Most of the time I'm at home or over at Sierra's house."

"Well, call me when you're out with Lyric and I can meet up with you. Mama doesn't let you date yet, does she?"

"Nope, not yet, but that doesn't stop me," I laughed.

"Oh, I got competition. That's messed up."

I pushed his shoulder playfully and told him to stop teasing me.

"Look, I got to meet up with some people, but I'll call you tonight. I promise."

I nodded my head in agreement and opened the door to get out. Slipping my sandals on, Carlos leaned in and gave me a hug. He kissed me on my cheek, and I wished it were my lips.

"You go to Hills High now, right?"

"Yeah."

"How about I call you and I come pick you up from school one day and we can just hang out?" I knew he meant to skip school. I hadn't done that before, though many of my friends had.

"That sounds good. Let me know when."

9

He hopped in his car, and I waved good-bye as he drove off. I decided to go find Lyric cause it was way past two in the morning. Finally, I spotted Kyra. "Hey, where's Lyric?"

"We were just about to go look for you. It's time to go; y'all are going to drop me off first."

"Okay, tell Lyric I'm going to the van." It was another ten minutes before Lyric came out with Johnny, a few of his friends, and Kyra. We all piled up in Mama's van and drove off. I sat way in the back because Johnny's friends reeked of smoke. I lay my head down and dreamed of Carlos like I used to years ago

They Called Her Lyric

"Cookie, I'm going to need you to hurry up in the bathroom. I got somewhere to go," Lyric yelled through the door.

Washing my hands I yelled back, "Where you going? Can I go?"

"Ain't anybody looking for your black ass. Get out of my way. Lynn just called, and we're going out." I opened the door, and Lyric pushed past me.

"Why can't I go? I ain't got anything to do." I remembered Carlos telling me to call him anytime I was with Lyric. I couldn't tell Lyric that because she would try any and everything for me not to see him. She did that just because.

Fixing her hair in the mirror she said, "You said you were bored last time, and I ain't got time to be hearing you bitch all night. Go watch TV or something."

Taking a chance I said, "Well, Carlos said he would meet me if I was with you."

Lyric started to laugh. Not the kind of laugh that you knew she felt something was funny, but the laugh where it meant she was laughing at you. "Girl, please. Carlos ain't thinking about you. He goes out with Sid."

"Sid? Since when?" Sid was a girl we used to hang out with. I hadn't seen her for a few years. Hearing this news hurt, but hearing it from Lyric's mouth cut my heart in two. This was another one of her ritual "say something to hurt Cookie's feelings."

Cookie

"I don't know, but I think that's where he was going when he left the party last weekend. You're too young for that boy anyway. Like I said, take your black ass in the living room and go watch TV."

"You better shut up talking to me like that. Your ass ain't bright either." I stormed away from the bathroom when she started to call me everything she could think of. I yelled a few insults her way before I closed my door and plopped down on my bed.

The tears stung my eyes as I faced reality that I was too young and that Carlos was not thinking about me. I wiped my tears away and looked at my bookshelf. Then I grabbed my journal, opened it up to the first blank page, and started to write.

> *Days like this I wish Lyric would get hit by a car. Her daily routine of "black bitch this," and "black ass that," and "you ugly as hell" comments are working my last nerve. You would think by now she'd have grown out of that phase. As if she was some supermodel or something. Her ass is 50 pounds heavier than mine. I just don't get why she can't leave me alone. If I could drive I wouldn't even bother going out with her. But Mama is always at work or watching TV, and since Jayla and Lola moved to Corpus Christi, the house has been empty to me. But you know what? I finally realized that I am not ugly like Lyric says I am. The boys at school say different, and I'm starting to believe them. I looked in the mirror the other day and for the first time in a long time I didn't cry. I think Lyric's words are starting not to hurt me anymore. Maybe this is the turning point. The*

moment I can live and not be under Lyric's shadow anymore. Maybe if I show her that I'm cute, her daily routine of insults will stop. I guess we will see, huh?

I placed my pen in the book and leaned back against my bedroom wall. Writing always helped me get my emotions out. I got tired of those suicidal thoughts that used to haunt me day and night. Growing up in church I knew suicide would take me straight to hell, so I had to find another way to ease the pain. Writing was my escape.

Don't get me wrong. I love my sister. But I love her just because she is my sister—but I still hate her. If we weren't blood, I wouldn't bother to look twice at her. She ain't never done anything nice for me anyhow but try to beat me down emotionally. Sometimes I wonder if Mama knows the depth of my hatred for Lyric. Maybe she started to learn the day Lyric threatened to kill me.

£££

It was like any normal day after church. Mama had to go for an errand, and Lynn and her cousin were over at our house. Our home used to be a revolving door for family, friends, and anyone in between. Mama just had a caring heart like that. As usual, when Lyric had company I had to stay clear of her room. I couldn't breathe around her, look in her direction, or attempt to talk to her. I was glad Lynn's cousin was there 'cause now I had someone to hang out with. The day was going good—until Lyric had to start her ritual again.

I heard Lyric's voice yell out to me. With our rooms right next door it wasn't hard to hear her conversation. I got up and walked over to her door and peeked in.

"Cookie, why are you always listening in on my business?"

"Lyric, you don't have any business." I slammed the door behind me and walked back to my room. Just because I had left didn't mean Lyric was done with her speech. Disregarding my privacy she barged in my room yelling her same accusations. "I was listening to her conversation," "I had been in her room," "she knew this" and "she knew that." This always worked my last nerve.

"Bitch, get out of my face and my room," I yelled back at her. By now, Lynn's cousin had got up and walked over to Lynn. I imagine she was telling her we were arguing. As usual I didn't know what the argument was about. I hopped off my bed before Lyric had the chance to pin me down.

"Oh, you bad now. You gonna step up to me?" Lyric screamed.

Truthfully, Lyric was a lot larger than my 120-pound frame. She was 175 pounds. But imagine a fist full of rage and just being fed up. That punch can pack a hard blow.

"Hey, y'all calm down. Lyric, go back to your room." Lynn tried to play the mediator.

Lyric reached out and pushed me back on my bed. "The next time I see you eavesdropping on me, I'm going to whoop your ass."

I was so angry I couldn't even hear the venom spitting out of my mouth. Every day Lyric had some new threat or insult for me, and I was fed up. I jumped up off my bed and pushed her back as she was walking out my door. "I hate you!" I screamed.

I guess me pushing back was a perfect reason for Lyric to turn around and punch me in my arm. This was maybe her 100th hit. I knew when we were going to fight before the blows actually took place. Why Lyric always wanted to fight me, I have no clue. But in all the fights I

14

never just stood there and took it. I pulled back with all my might and •
bunched Lyric right in the breast. She bellowed over, holding her chest,
and head butted me. *Are we sumo wrestlers now?* I fell to the floor
kicking in each and every direction I could. Lynn's protest to stop yet
another fight didn't work. I screamed out, "I hate you," over and over
again. I thought blood was spewing from my mouth. Lyric turned
around and ran down the hallway.

"I'm going to kill you, bitch, and then we'll see who's bad,"
Lyric hollered out.

"Lyric, calm down. Y'all two stop. Y'all are sisters. You
shouldn't be fighting like this." Lynn tried to overpower our voices as
she tried to help me up.

"Do it, bitch; cut me, ho. I want your fat ass to cut me." I
followed suit and sprinted to the living room. I saw Lyric pull out a
large butcher knife. *I wish she would cut me with that knife. Better yet,
I'm going to show her who's boss.*

Lyric ran toward me, and I dodged her and jumped in the
kitchen, where I pulled out the kitchen drawer full of cooking utensils. I
moved huge spoons and mixers out of the way in search of a knife like
the one she had. *Yes, this will do.* I swung out a silver, stainless steel
knife the length of a baby's arm and screamed, "Now what?"

"Put that down. I'm about to call y'all mama," Lynn
screamed. Her cousin had run to the back. I guess she didn't want to get
accidently stabbed.

"I can't stand you and your black ass." Lyric walked up to me,
and I spun around and placed the knife in front of me. I gripped its
wooden handle so hard the sweat started to drip from my hands. My
heart began to race as I faced my enemy. I wanted so much for her to

just go away. For my life to finally get easier. *Lord, I need this. If you just lead my hand to end her life, I promise you afterward I will never kill another soul. But she must die.*

We stood there nose to nose with our chests huffing and puffing every second of the minute. Rage had always caused both of us to lose our breath.

"Cut me!" I screamed.

"You cut me!" Lyric yelled back. This routine went on for five minutes when I realized I wasn't gonna stab her first. She had to be the reason why I killed her. I started to see that she wasn't gonna take my life.

"I knew you were all talk. Like I said, get the hell out of my face," I shouted, still holding the knife and walking away from what could have been the day we both committed murder. Lynn couldn't stop this from happening nor could her cousin. I hated Lyric, and one day she would know why.

£££

"OK, get your stuff. You can roll with us," Lyric said, peeping her head in my door and taking my thoughts away from that day.

"For real?" I said, jumping up, already searching for something to wear.

"Yeah, now hurry up and don't make me change my mind."

I ran to my closet and pulled out a new skirt Mama had just bought me and a spaghetti strapped shirt that showed just above my navel. I grabbed my hair mousse out of my hair bag, sprayed some in my hands, and smoothed it over my new braids. I didn't know what we were going to do tonight, but I wanted to have fun.

£££

16

I looked out the passenger-side window and noticed Lynn walking out with her boo in tow. Lynn was a friend of the family. She had been friends with Lyric and Jayla since middle school. Up until a few years ago, our house had five women living in it. It was me, Lyric, Jayla, and Lola, who is my godmother. When Lola got married to Jayla's father, they all moved to Corpus Christi, which is six hours away from Fort Worth. Life changed after that, and not for the better.

"All right, Cookie, get in the back." I pulled open the sliding door of the van.

"Damn, Lyric, is that little Cookie?" Lynn's boo asked.

"Who in the hell you looking at? Get your ass back in the house," Lynn yelled in jealousy. I rolled my eyes and crawled into the back of the van. I was never interested in the guys they liked anyhow.

Lyric pulled out and said, "We going to Woodlake to hang out."

"For what? To see Johnny? That's for you," Lynn protested. I agreed. No one wanted to hang out just to watch them kiss all night.

"No, girl, Johnny got some friends with him. I'm sure you can find you somebody to chill with."

"What about me?" I whined.

"You too, Cook. It'll be fun. Just watch."

We pulled into Woodlake Apartments right off of Highway 30 and at the edge of Woodhaven, an area in Fort Worth. It wasn't the best area to hang out at, but it was cool. Most black folks lived on this side of town. I never knew what it meant to have black neighbors. All of ours were white.

"Do you see him?" Lynn asked. Lyric parked the van and pulled out her cell phone to call Johnny. Two minutes later, he and

17

three other guys walked out. I noticed a few of his friends. *Hey, that one's cute.* Lyric got out, and so did Lynn. Shy as always, I leaned back in the seat and pulled out a book. This just wasn't my type of scenery.

"Who's that in the back?" I heard one of Johnny's friends ask.

"Oh, that's Cook. She's Lyric's sister," Johnny said.

"Cook?"

"Cook is short for Cookie," Lynn corrected them. I leaned up to see who was so interested to find out who was in the van. He was tall, maybe six foot, curly hair, and had a baby face. *Dang, he is fine.*

"Lynn, I'm about to go see Johnny's sister. Take them to go get some flavored cigars, will ya?" I saw Lyric hand Lynn the keys and walk off with Johnny. I hated when she did that because Mama always said don't let anybody else drive this van. I saw the tall one pull back the sliding door, and I sat up immediately, not wanting him to see my thighs or anything else. He sat down in the row in front of me, and the other guy hopped in the passenger seat.

"Hey, Cookie. I'm Baron. That's my brother Kevin."

"Hey," I shyly said.

I leaned back and stared out the window as Lynn pulled the van out of the parking lot. They drove up to the nearest corner store where Lynn and Kevin got out.

"Lynn, crack the windows, will ya?" I yelled before she left. I wanted some air to take away this Texas heat.

It didn't take long for Baron to start up with a conversation that I wasn't interested in having. I always gave guys attitude just because.

"So, you and Lyric are sisters? Y'all look just alike."

"So I've been told."

18

"What school you go to?"

"Hills High, and you?"

"I'm in a GED program at Trimble. Almost done too."

Dang, he's older than I thought he was.

"Oh yeah? How's that coming along?"

"Not as hard as I thought but can't wait to be done. I dropped out, but my mama made me go back for the GED."

"Oh yeah? So that makes you how old?"

"Eighteen. I'll be nineteen in a few months. What about you?"

"What about me?"

"How old are you?"

"Too young."

He laughed off my remark. I thought I certainly was giving him attitude. I didn't see anything funny.

"Dang, Cookie, why you so mean? Loosen up. I don't bite. You may even like me."

"We'll see." I leaned back in my seat and pulled out a book I was reading by Omar Tyree. By this time, Lynn and Kevin were back and started up the car. We headed back to Woodlake Apartments. I wasn't a fool enough to sit in a hot car in the middle of April, so I hopped out with everyone else following suit.

"Where we going?" I asked, clearly bored and irritated.

"Over by the pool area. Come on, you can roll with me." Baron tried to put his arm around my shoulder, but I said no thanks. I didn't know him that well to be all hugged up by him.

I saw a group of guys and girls over by the pool, and Lyric was in the blend. I always felt that Lyric and I were privileged and that we were raised proper and segregated from the black society. So I

19

guess this is why every time Lyric got the chance to go to the hood she went.

I walked over and found a bench to sit on and pulled out my book again. *Oh yeah, I should call Carlos.* "Lyric, let me use your phone really quick."

Surprisingly, without hesitation, she held her phone out toward me. I guess because Johnny had her occupied. I walked over and got it and went back to the bench, punching his numbers in at the same time.

Ring!

"Hello," I heard him say.

"Carlos, hey, it's me."

After a long pause he said, "Me who?"

Trying to not sound disappointed I said, "Cookie!"

"Oh, hey, Cook, what's up?"

Seeing this was not going to be a conversation I wanted to go my way I said, "I'm out with Lyric and wanted to know if you could meet me."

"Where are you at?"

"I'm in Woodhaven in Woodlake Apartments, and it's right off Sandy Lane and Highway 30."

"Oh yeah, I know a few dudes out that way. I may come by. Let me holla back at you, a'ight?"

More crushed than anything, I flipped the phone shut and placed it in my pocket without saying good-bye. I was not going to get excited about him back in my life when it was obvious I wasn't what was on his mind.

I noticed a boy I used to have a crush on walk my way. "Hey, Cookie, I ain't seen you in a while. We about to dance. Wanna get down?"

"Hey, Mark, not really in the mood to."

"Aw, come on. You too pretty to be looking all sad and like someone just killed your best friend. Come on and dance with me." He reached out and brushed my hand with his. Just then, Dru Hill's latest hit came over the stereo someone had sitting out in their apartment window. I couldn't resist the temptation to dance to one of my favorite songs.

"OK, Mark, but stay off my booty," I said, taking his hand and following him to a more open area.

I was not the best dancer at all. I felt my hips went one way while my legs went the other. I just knew the standard dance. Stick my butt out, roll it around, and bounce. I was bouncing to the beat, and Mark was grinding on my hips. I started to get disgusted because I wasn't feeling him like that to be so close up on me. I moved to create some space. As my body went in another direction I turned my head and noticed Baron watching me. *What is he staring at? He's making me uncomfortable.*

I noticed Lynn was really getting to know Kevin literally. I looked over also and saw Johnny and Lyric deep into each other's mouths. "Whew, OK, Mark, I'm officially tired. I'm going to go sit down. Get at me later." He didn't like the fact I left him dancing in midair, but my thighs hurt from trying to bounce too hard. Plus, I felt I was making a fool of myself.

"So you and Mark, huh?"

I looked up and noticed Baron standing over me. *What's up with this dude? He sure does know how to crowd your space. Ugh.*

"Oh no, we just friends. Why? What's up with you?" He took a seat next to me.

"Nothing; you just seem cool to talk to, that's all."

"Yeah, OK. We haven't said but two words to each other. There are plenty of females here for you to drool over."

"Dang, Cookie, why are you so mean? You got a man or something?"

Ugh, I heard that question at the age of fourteen so much I was sure that I would hear it a thousand times before I hit eighteen. "Baron, right? Look, you seem cool. But you are way too old for me to be trying to kick it with."

"Why do you assume that's what I want? Maybe I was looking for a conversation." Not trying to roll my eyes too hard, I listened to his sob story. "You sure know how to tear a brother down."

"I'm not trying to be rude or nothing like that, but most of y'all ain't about nothing. I don't have time for all that."

"You talk as if you're thirty."

"I'm fourteen, and what's your point?"

"Wow, fourteen. You sure don't seem like you're fourteen."

"Oh, I am so sure." I was done with the conversation.

"Look, I just want to be friends, that's all. You cool with that?"

"Baron, answer me this." I leaned forward as if I were getting ready to whisper something to him. "Why the interest in being my friend?"

He started to look around the crowd. The scene wasn't pretty at all. Girls half dressed with breasts and butt cheeks hanging out dancing in uncut grass where paper cups that used to have alcohol in them decorated the ground. Music was blasting from an old boom box someone set in their window, and the pool was full of dirty leaves. Then it hit me. I was mad right now because I was sitting in filth. I hated going to the hood. It was never clean. "You see them?" He pointed to three girls with ten-inch nails that were colored a hot pink and purple and hair so tall they could beat Kid's box from Kid N Play.

"Yeah, what about them?"

"Now do you see them over there?" He pointed in the opposite direction, and I saw two guys dancing on one girl as they made a sandwich out of her. Nothing on her body was untouched as they grabbed and plucked on every curve of her body.

"Yeah, I see them. What about them?" I said, shrugging my shoulders.

"Now look at you." I started to feel a little insecure as I started to examine my outfit.

"What?"

"I would rather take interest in a girl like you any day. Plus, I see you aren't too easy to talk to, which makes it more of a pleasure to talk with a girl who knows who she wants to be with."

"So now you know me, huh?"

"No, but I badly want to. I know you may think I'm too old. But friends are all I'm asking for." He extended his hand for me to shake. "So we cool?"

I smiled as he started to grow on me. "Yeah, we cool." I took his hands in mine and pulled out my book. I wanted to tell him about

23

the girl in the story who just met this older guy and started to fall head over heels for him.

He joked and said, "How did that author know our future already? That's amazing."

I laughed and pushed his shoulder in an effort to flirt.

"Baron, right? OK, yeah, we can be friends."

A Mother's A Keeper

"No, no, Mama, that's not how you do it," I said, grabbing the remote to change the station to the basketball game.

"Go get me some popcorn and take my jug and get me some water." I took her water jug to fill it again for the tenth time today.

"Mama, can you please put on some clothes. If I am going to be sitting in here, I ain't trying to see all that," I laughed. She yelled down the hallway and repeated for me to bring her water and popcorn.

I went into the cabinet to find one of her light butter popcorn bags. I filled her jug full of ice all the way to the top as she liked it and poured water over it. Then the phone rang.

Ring!

"Hello," I said.

"Hey, Cookie, how you doing?"

"Oh, hey, Aunt Flo, how you doing?" Aunt Flo was my mother's sister who stayed right around the corner. She was my favorite aunt who I used to spend at least one day a week over at her house until I started to want to do older things with Lyric.

"I'm good. Just home and school as always."

"That's good, baby. Put Della on the phone for me, wills ya?" I yelled down the hall for Mama to pick up the phone. When I heard her end pick up, I slid the phone back in its cradle.

Lyric walked in the kitchen. "What y'all about to do?"

"Me and mama about to watch the Mavericks game and eat popcorn. You ain't going out tonight?"

"Yeah, Tony is about to come pick me up." She walked over to the refrigerator. Tony was another male friend of Lyric's. One I

25

didn't bother to know or ask about. I grabbed the hot bag of popcorn out of the microwave and walked back into Mama's room.

She had hung up with Aunt Flo already.

"What did Aunt Flo want?"

"Nothing." When Mama cut the conversation short about her sisters it was usually because they asked for something and she didn't want me to fuss over it. Mama had four sisters that count and two who were taken away from my grandmother as babies back in the '50s. She also had five brothers. I would be saying it lightly if I said our family was big.

"OK, Mama, I hope you told her we are broke."

"Shut up, Cookie, and hand me my damn popcorn." I surrendered the food that she wanted and slid down on the floor next to her bed to watch the game. When it came to protesting giving somebody in our family money I said no. Mainly because with Mama only getting SSI and working every hour that her body allowed her to, we were still pinching dollars. I didn't realize we had so little money until I got older. She never let this show when we were kids.

"Mama, I'm for real. Tell her no." She didn't reply. I reached in and grabbed some of her popcorn. I had to look for the popcorn bag blind because I refused to turn around. Mama loved to lay naked, and at over 350 pounds, I always begged her to wear a shirt or something. But home is where you were supposed to let loose, and she did just that.

"Who do you think is going to win tonight?" I asked, stuffing a fistful of popcorn in my mouth.

"You know I am going for Nash." He was Mama's favorite player on the Mavericks basketball team.

"Oh yeah, Mama, I forgot to mention that the other day I ran into Carlos."

"Oh really? Where did you see him at?" She held sarcasm in her voice as she hoped that I spilled the beans of Lyric's and my whereabouts.

"We were at Lynn's house, and he just popped over there. He is all grown up too. He has his own car and everything."

"Well, I guess since he left Bishop's house he can do just about anything."

I shrugged my shoulders and said, "I guess so. But anyways, he wanted to know if he could come over and visit and you make those beans and corn bread."

She laughed out and said, "Hell, that boy used to eat up all my food. Now he want some more."

My mother was like most neighborhood mothers back in the day. Her door was always open; she cooked food and anyone could eat it; and she would be just a call away when you needed advice. I wouldn't say I was just the opposite, but sometimes I did wish she held a mean bone in her body. It seemed that even if someone used her, she wouldn't wish anything for them but the best. I guess that can be a good thing.

I remember this one time when on one of those rare occasions I asked about my daddy. The title itself didn't move me because in my world I didn't have a daddy. He lived less than ten miles away from me, and I never saw him. I could count on one hand the times he visited. I could also count on one hand the amount of Christmas gifts or birthday presents I got. Not even a phone call. *Sorry* wouldn't even explain the type of man he was.

27

Even when Mama opened up only a twenty-dollar child support check, she didn't curse his name. When our lights were cut off or we didn't have any cable, she didn't curse or wish bad things upon him. My mother honestly never said one bad word about my daddy.

Now if that isn't a kindhearted woman, then I don't know what is.

"Yeah, he can come over. But y'all stay in the living room." I jumped up and hugged her and gave her a sloppy kiss on the cheek. "Get off me, girl," she laughed and wiped her face. I took another handful of popcorn and turned the volume up on the game.

£££

I took Mama's JPS certification card and went to stand in line to check her name in. The clinic was newly built adjacent to the John Peter Smith County Hospital where I and most of my family were born. It was pretty nice. The walls were clean, and the carpet was fresh. I hated going to the older clinic. The central air rarely worked, and the waiting area was always crowded with sick folks and crying babies I didn't care to hear.

I got up to the counter and told the receptionist that I was checking in Della James. She confirmed the appointment and told me to have Mama go into the nurse's station to have blood drawn. I nodded my head, displaying that I knew the routine. This was only maybe my 30th time bringing her in.

I had to get used to the needles, understanding the medical chitchat, and dodging the old folks who wore the Depends and couldn't tell when they needed to be changed. This was a routine at fourteen I wish I didn't know. But Mama was a diabetic and had high blood pressure too. To top that off, she had to have breathing treatments

28

because she would stop breathing in her sleep. When I found out about the congestive heart failure, I wondered how much worse it could get.

The nurses were used to me asking questions about what they were doing and why they poked her here and there. I guess this was my responsibility now. Lyric used to do it, but then her priorities changed dramatically.

"Cookie, help me up." I took Mama's arm and wrapped it around my tiny waist to give her a boost on her feet. I followed her into the nurse's station for her regular blood work. The news was always the same. It never changed. "Blood pressure still high." "Here, take this medicine. It'll help this and don't forget to take it. It will help." Yada yada. I nodded my head as I listened about the medicine and directions given to me in alphabetical order.

I was surprised this time at how quick we were in and out. *Only two hours this time. If we hurry up, I can go watch my shows.* "Mama, can you drop me off over at Sierra's house? I think her mama is going to drop us off at the bowling alley tonight."

"Yeah, what else y'all gonna do?" She teased me with the usual interrogation.

"Nothing. That's it, I think. Why? You going to be bored at the house?"

"Naw, I may go over to Flo's house, and then back home to watch the game."

"OK, well, you can call me if you get bored, and I'll come on home."

"I'll be all right. You and Lyric always seem like you two too busy these days."

29

"What do you mean we hanging out now? It's Lyric who is always MIA."

"She acts just like Howard did when he was her age. She too much of a people person; always think she got to be in the crowd."

"Well, that was you too, Mama. She just likes to have friends. All I need is a good book, TV, food, and a closed room and I'm good. Have you talked to Howard, I mean, Daddy, lately anyhow?"

"Nope, why? You want to talk to him? Call him."

"No thanks, I'll pass." She breathed a sigh and got on to Highway 20 straight to Sierra's house. The conversation about Howard was usually short and to the point. He was my daddy not my father, and believe me, there's a difference. I hopped out of the van but not before kissing Mama on the cheek, and walked up to Sierra's house.

Two Peas in A Pod

I wasn't ten feet away when she pushed opened her screen door and said, "Come on in, slut. I got some juice."

I waved off her nickname and walked in the front door. "What gossip you got now?"

"I heard Trent at school wants to holler at you."

"So what? I already told that fool he ain't my type. I don't do athletes. They always think they all that. Plus, he seemed to like white girls anyhow."

"That's not what Lisa's cousin Trina, who is friends with Jessica, who is Brandon's girlfriend, who is best friends with Trent, said."

I rolled my eyes at this confusing time line of names she just rolled out her mouth. Sierra was my only friend since second grade. Other than her, no one was labeled my friend. I was what you called an outcast. "Sierra, please gives it a rest. That boy ain't got nothing I want."

"Well, I got his phone number," she boasted.

"Why and how?" I plopped down on her bed which was smothered with plush pillows that were pink and green. Her room held the ambiance of a flower garden. She was obsessed with flowers, and if you stared too long at her floral wall pattern, your eyes started to go in a hypnotized daze.

"Friday he gave it to me. I wasn't able to give it to you then because you had gone out with Lyric and Lynn, but not today. Today, you gonna call ole dude."

I took the number and crumbled it up in my hand and threw it across the room into her trash can.

"Ugh, ho, why did you do that?"

"Sisi, if you don't stop calling me your sisterly bond names I'm gonna whoop your ass." The words *bitch, ho, slut, tramp,* and any other women-demoting names were some of Sierra's favorite words in the dictionary. "I told you that Carlos is back."

"His fine ass ain't checking for you, and Trent is fine."

"Trent is self-centered. I don't like guys who have a bubble head and an IQ of an ape."

"Well, who are you into then? 'Cause I am so into David, and he's meeting us tonight at the bowling alley. He's bringing some friends."

"Ugh, you invited him and his posse? He's probably bringing his dorky-ass friend. He was drooling over my shoulder the last time. I'm gonna call Mama to come and get me. You just ruined my night."

"Aw, come on. I mean, you don't have anyone you can call to meet us there?"

I thought about calling Carlos because who else would there be? Baron crossed my mind, but I didn't even have his number and besides, since the one time we talked, I haven't spoken to him since. "OK, I'll call Carlos and see if he wants to meet me down there."

Ring!

"Carlos, how are you?"

"Hey, Cookie, I'm sorry about last time. I was so busy, and then time got away."

"You know me. I don't really care about any lame excuse you got. But I called to see if you wanted to meet up. Sierra and I are going to Don Carters. I didn't want to be solo."

"Yeah, tonight, that sounds cool. I got a couple guys who can go. You got some more friends?" he said. I heard a lot of guys' voices in the background.

"Wow, how many are over there?"

"Four, and I am on my way to come and get you."

I didn't feel comfortable riding with a bunch of guys, and if the shoe were on the other foot, Sierra would have jumped headfirst to do it. "No, Sierra's sister is dropping us off. You can meet us there." Sierra started waving her hands in the background, trying to get me to change my mind about the ride.

"Tell him yes," she whispered. I waved her off and pushed her away from the phone. I hung up before Sierra got the urge to grab the phone.

"Calm down. He had a pack of boys with him, and you know I don't roll like that. Let me call Lyric and see if she and Lynn want to come."

"Yeah, because you know Lyric always rolls deep with the new potential boyfriends." I laughed and waved Sierra off who was always boy crazy.

"Hey, Cook, what's up?"

I heard loud music in the background and a car full of people.

"Who are you riding with?"

"We in Johnny's mama's car. What's up?"

"I was calling to see if y'all want to meet us at Don Carters. Everybody is going to be there tonight."

4

"Hey, Kyra, you want to go to Don Carter's?" I heard Lyric ask her other best friend.

"Hey, Cookie, we'll meet you there. Who are you riding with?"

"Sierra and her sister. I'll see you there." I hung up and ran to Sierra's mirror to start fixing my hair. Sierra passed me her pink lip gloss, and I spread some across my lips and was satisfied with my look.

£££

The bowling alley was packed. It was the play pen for youngins who were too young to go to the club. I was swishing my hips from side to side feeling like I was a million bucks. My outfit was perfect. My butt was round and looked curvaceous in my jeans, and my toe ring sparkled on my middle toe. My long, jet-black hair was down in loose curls and swayed with each step I took.

"Oh, you think you da bomb now. I see you walking all high and mighty," Sierra teased. "Oh, hey, look, there's David." She pulled my arm and forced me to follow her. As I suspected, he had the wolf pack with him.

"Hey, boo." She leaned in and gave David a hug. He hugged her a little too tight, and his hands were planted right above her butt. I rolled my eyes in annoyance.

David looked over toward me with that sex stare I hated to see in boys I didn't like. "Hey, Cookie. You know the guys, right?"

"Yeah. Hey, I'll be back. Going to go get me a Sprite."

Sierra yelled after me, "Get me one too."

As I squeezed through the crowd I felt someone grab my hand and swing me into their body. Before I could reject the offer, I was in his embrace. He whispered in my ear, "I been thinking about you."

5

I looked up and said, "Baron, what are you doing here?"

"I came with Lyric and Kyra. They're around here somewhere. I was just looking for you. Been thinking about you since last weekend. You look nice."

I finally let loose of his hands and regained my composure before I was whisked away like Cinderella. I had to take a double look because homeboy was looking extra fine tonight. I mean, I didn't know much about ole dude but his plump, pink lips, silky, curly hair, and his to-die-for cocoa-brown skin made me melt. I couldn't help but fall like putty in his hands.

"Well, it's good to see you." I was a little confused with his ear-to-ear smile. Why was he so excited to see me? A girl he barely knew.

"Where were you going?"

"To get me and my girl something to drink."

"Cool. I'll walk with ya. I'll get it for you." As if I needed him to buy me some sodas. I didn't object to the offer though. We walked through the crowd and toward the food counter. The guy in the pin-striped shirt smiled a little too hard toward me. I guess Baron sensed the filtration. *All dogs think alike.*

"Hey, let me get three Sprites, a large popcorn, and Cookie, you want something else?"

Of course I want something else. It's free for me. "Let me get a hot dog and a pickle." He rang up our order, and we walked off with our items in tow. The crowd seemed as if it thickened with each passing second. I spotted Sierra sitting next to David. *I thought she was coming to bowl not mack.*

6

"Hey, Cookie, is this for me?" Sierra asked, knowing already this was for her. She wanted to interrogate me about Baron.

"Yeah, Sierra, here's your soda."

She pulled my arm and said, "Girl, either Carlos done changed or he has a twin." She pointed her head away from me and signaled for me to turn around.

No, no, no, this couldn't be happening. "Hey, Carlos, you made it." The soda in my hand almost dropped. I took a long gulp because suddenly my mouth became bone-dry.

"Hey, Cook, I promised you, right?" he leaned in and kissed me on my forehead like he would normally do. Baron cleared his throat as if he had something to say about this odd situation.

Bad karma must have told God to play one of the most emotional songs on earth, "Don't Ask My Neighbor" by The Emotions, because it immediately came on. I could have slapped the DJ right now. He must have known about my double date that apparently was about to hit an all-time low.

"Hey, what's your name?" Sierra asked Baron. He replied and she said, "Let me holla at you for a minute."

I am too young to be going through this dilemma.

"Am I missing something?" Carlos asked. Wanting to get away from David and his wolf pack, I asked Carlos to follow me over to the nearest open table. It wasn't easy walking through a crowd where you rubbed up against everyone. I was so happy that Sierra took Baron away.

I set my soda and hot dog down on the table and took a minute to compose myself. "Sierra had to dismiss a friend, that's all. Double booking."

"Double booking. As if in that's your new man?"

"No, he is a new friend who hangs out with Lyric, and she didn't tell me he was coming. Are you cool with that?" I openly asked. Although the situation was awkward, I did not want to feel like I did something wrong.

"Dang, Cook, I knew you were fine as hell, but you sure got a brother competing for your attention."

"No, you're cool. I mean, it ain't like you were calling me anyhow."

"Well, I'll make sure I don't slip up. I don't want to be pushed to the back of the line."

I laughed and bit into my hot dog. Maybe this was the situation he needed to see for him to take me seriously. I needed to be a priority if he wanted to talk to me and actually spend time together.

After I finished my hot dog we walked back over toward David and his crew. They were entering in the names for a bowling match in the computer. I teamed up with David and Sierra, and Carlos and decided to let the night move past that awkward moment. But in the back of my mind I thought about Baron and how he must be feeling about my dismissing him. I wasn't the type to be that rude to someone, although I couldn't help the situation.

I let one game of bowling go by, then I took off to go find Lyric and the rest of the gang. I told Carlos I had to use the bathroom. I had taken off before he could reply. I rushed through the crowd as if ants were attacking my feet. I searched high and low and decided to look upstairs in the pool area. I had to dodge the usual wannabe mack daddies that thought I was twenty verses my jail-bait age of fourteen.

I spotted Kyra and a sigh of relief left my lungs as I noticed Johnny, and then Lyric. It was Baron who I couldn't yet see. "Hey, Kyra and Lyric."

"Hey, Cookie, we was wondering where you were," Kyra said.

"Where's Baron?"

"You mean fine-ass Baron who was dissed by Little Miss Cookie?" Kyra tried to pat my shoulder like I was a puppy. I dodged her hand and her rude comment.

"Yes, that Baron. Where is he?"

"You looking for me?" I heard a deep voice from behind me. His sudden appearance scared me, and I jumped in reaction to his voice.

"Hey, I need to talk to you." I reached for his hand, but he didn't reach back. *Ugh, he better not give me attitude. I'm trying to be nice.*

"Didn't you just kick him to the curb for pretty boy Carlos?" Lyric blurted out. Not surprised from her comment, I rolled my eyes and asked Baron again to follow me to a more private area. Of course he refused. *What are we now, twelve or something?*

"OK, I wanted to come check on you, Baron, but this is ridiculous. I didn't do anything wrong, and you have no reason to act jealous or mad. We said we were friends, right?"

"Yeah, whatever you say." He walked past me but not before bumping me on the shoulder.

This nigga here is about to get slapped.

I shrugged my shoulders and said, "Whatever. Some friend you are, huh, Baron?" I turned and jogged down the steps to hurry back toward Carlos before I had two mad boys on my hands.

My trail back to Carlos was stopped abruptly by the ever-growing crowd. I felt my hand be grabbed from behind. I snatched it away, frightened by the touch more than anything. I whisked around and noticed it was Baron. *Really, you GOT to be kidding me.*

"I'm sorry, and you're right. I'm acting mad for no reason, and I'm sorry."

"That's all I wanted to hear. You wanted to be my friend, remember? Well, be that and not make me feel bad for having other friends. This situation is ridiculous, and I don't want to make this a routine."

"I got you. I just wanted to say I'm sorry." I gave him a small hug and told him I would talk to him later and to give Lyric his number for me to call.

As I got near Sierra and the gang I noticed Carlos talking on his phone. David's friends had branched out, and I could spot a few talking to girls and exchanging phone numbers. That was the usual scene at Don Carter's.

"I'm back."

"Had to go check on ole dude, huh?"

He had said that with an attitude, and I wasn't in the mood with another interrogation. What was up with these guys? We weren't in a relationship. He rose up out of his seat and took my hand in his and asked me to follow him. I did without hesitation, wondering what he had up his sleeve. I yelled back to Sierra that I would be right back.

We ended up at his car. He opened his passenger-side door. He asked, "When do you have to be back at the bowling alley?"

10

"Eleven," I said clueless. He closed my side of the door and walked around and hopped in the driver's seat. Then he cranked the engine.

"Where are we going?"

"Just for a ride. Don't you want to just get away and talk?"

I nodded my head in agreement as he pulled out of the parking lot, wondering if I was making a mistake.

£££

The Brooks Lake was the largest body of water on our side of town. The sight of it at night was my most favorite thing about it. During the day you would see many boats and families with their barbecue pits ready to seize the moment. But not tonight. It was only a little after nine and not a soul in sight. Carlos parked his car, and we headed toward the hill. Once you reached the top of it, you would see the entire lake and the moon beaming directly on the middle of it.

"I remember when we came here with Higher Touch, just us kids; and when the only thing that was on our minds was Higher Touch and being all good and shit. Do you remember that?" Carlos asked. Higher Touch was our church from back in the day. It was the only church I had attended since the age of three.

"Who wouldn't? It was our home away from home. Now you don't know where any of the old church members are. Do you miss it?"

He looked at me as if I had asked him the worst question in the world. "Not at all."

"Is it because of Bishop?"

"Well, don't get me wrong. I do miss seeing you all the time. You are what made me get through all that. Not being able to have friends, go to a public school, or talk on the phone. I hated that house."

11

"I'm sorry you had to go through that," I said rubbing his shoulders. "I do miss it though. It was my home away from home. I know if I was there again I would feel more connected to you," I stuttered. "I just don't think I know you any more."

He turned his head away from me, I guess to hide his reaction. I wanted to know what he felt. How he felt about me now.

"I know we're too young to feel like this. But you can't help who you are drawn to, right?" he asked.

"I guess not."

"Do you remember the day I had Deray bring you to the back of the church?"

Jogging my memory I said, "Oh yeah, the day I let you kiss me."

He laughed. "Yeah, that. I didn't do it right the first time. I guess after four years of wondering how your lips would feel on mine I got too anxious."

"What do you mean?"

"Was it your first time?"

Too embarrassed to admit it, I looked away. I didn't want him to view me as a girl. I wanted to seem like a woman.

"I'm sorry I didn't take my time. I guess kissing in the back of the church you don't have much time to do it right."

"Yes, that was the point, wasn't it?"

We found a spot soft enough for a cushion in the grass at the top of the hill and sat down. "Do you come here a lot or something?" I asked picking up a daisy and twirling it around in my fingers.

"Yeah, it's my favorite place to think. About the past, the future, and you know, you."

12

Curious to what he thought I asked, "You want to tell me what it is you are thinking about me?"

I felt his warm breath trail across my cheeks as the night's cool air blew. All of a sudden, my body got real hot, as if I were sitting on top of an oven burner. My insides began to release a heated sensation and started to pulsate wildly. Carlos leaned in even closer as my breathing began to get rapid. *What is this feeling? I feel like I'm going to explode.* I couldn't help the tension that was between us right now as he gently placed his lips on my cheek. He moved his hand up to my face to turn it toward his. Unable to speak and with a dry mouth, he placed his lips on top of mine.

Not a pro at kissing, I followed his lead with opening my mouth just a little so that his lips could fit perfectly with mine. The soft connection of his lips on mine suddenly made my insides boil over. I jumped back breathing heavily. "No, that is not what you did in the back of the church."

"No, you see, here, I can take my time." He leaned in for my lips again as something in between my legs started to throb. *What is that?* I didn't want to look down and search for whatever in the world was making me jump inside like that.

A moan escaped my mouth, and I pulled back and covered my mouth in embarrassment. "I am so sorry, Carlos. I don't do this with just anyone."

He leaned back to his side and breathed out. Finally, he looked down at his hands and said, "I'm going to stop because I want this to be different. Can you promise me something?" he looked over toward me as I tried to study his expression.

"Yeah, what is it?"

13

"Promise me that you will only allow me to kiss you that way. I want to be with you, Cookie, but the right way. We have been back and forth like this most of lives now. Let's just do it right the first time."

I nodded my head in agreement, still wondering what it was that we just did. I was sure I would find out in more detail soon.

Tamika Newhouse

Tell Me It's Real

"I can't hear you, Sisi, speak up," I whispered into the phone. I could hear her moaning and weeping, but I couldn't make out anything else. In South Hills you aren't allowed to have a cell phone in class. I did happen to forget that mine was on vibration. I saw Sierra's number and wondered how she was calling me if she was supposed to be in class.

I raised my hand and said, "Ms. Jones, can I go to the bathroom, please?" I got the pass and ran into the girls' bathroom and pulled out my cell phone. I only had it for a week, and I had to beg Mama to get it for me.

"Sisi, is that you? Speak up. I can't understand you."

"Cook, come get me, please. I don't know exactly where I am," she cried out. I could hear her sniffle into the phone.

"Wait, what do you mean? Where are you? Are you on campus?"

"Yes, somewhere down the choir hall, past old man Thomas's room."

"Why are you back there? That part of the school is closed. Nothing is back there."

"I know. I was stupid. He said he just wanted to talk, and I followed him. I don't know where I am."

Confused, I said, "What do you mean? It's like ten rooms back there with no electricity. Who would you follow back there?"

"David."

Getting upset, I said, "David? Why and what did y'all do? Wait, why are you crying? Sisi, what happened?"

16

She started to cry hysterically now, and I could hardly make out what she was saying as her phone started to break up. "He made me do it. I didn't want to, and when I screamed, he hit me with something, and I can't see anything. I don't know ..."

Her phone cut off.

Looking at the phone with tears in my eyes I tried redialing her number. It went straight to voice mail. I opened the bathroom stall and slammed the door back, running down the hallway. I heard one of the hall monitors yell for me to stop running in the hall.

Yeah, right. Make me stop. I ran down the first flight of stairs and ended up on the second floor. Quickly, I went down the second hall and started to search for the science room.

I saw Trent walk toward me and say, "Hey, Cookie, you're looking fine as hell today."

Breathing heavily I said, "Where's your boy at?"

"Who?" Trent asked confused.

"I don't have time for this. Where the hell is David? I want to see him."

"He's in the gym."

I rushed past him bumping his shoulder in the process. I heard Trent yell from behind asking me what was wrong, and I could tell he had started running after me.

Not wanting anyone to keep me from reaching that gym, I sped up. I was a fast runner having run track last semester, and only quitting because I didn't want to do the crucial training. I saw another hall monitor yell out to me to stop running, and then I heard Trent yell to him.

"Something's going on."

17

A few of the sophomore girls had yelled out, "Where's everybody running to?" I looked back behind me and saw at least five people following me. I turned the corner as quickly as I could and jumped down four steps at a time trying to reach the gym. I knew more than ever I had to make it to the gym before someone stopped me. I made it to the bottom floor and ran past the auditorium. Then I saw the gym doors and a girl in a volleyball uniform walked out.

"Move out of the way!" I screamed. She jumped out of my path as I swung open the door.

"David!" I screamed so loudly that my voice bounced off the walls. The coach blew the whistle as I walked breathing heavily onto the court.

"Latoya, you are going to have to get off the court," my old coach said to me. I hated when he refused to call me Cookie.

Not wanting anyone to lead me out of the gym I screamed at David, "You fucking raped her. Where is Sierra? Take me to her, you bitch. I'm going to cut you so deep. You want to rape somebody, come at me right now. I'll make a man out of you. Take me to her." My eyes were swollen with tears as they started to burn down my face.

I heard teammates start to fidget and repeat my announcement. I wasn't ashamed to tell the world of what he supposedly did. I wanted him to pay. Never again will I keep my mouth shut and not say anything.

Coach walked up to me and said, "Latoya, what did you just say?"

I noticed David trying to inch out of the gym. "Coach, catch him. He raped Sierra and locked her up somewhere in the band hall."

18

Coach swung around toward David, who was throwing up his hands in surrender trying to come up with a lie.

"Coach, she's lying. I don't know what the hell she's talking about."

"Yo', David, you told me you got that bruise from the ball," one of David's classmates yelled out.

Coach yelled, "What bruise? Son, you better tell me what is going on and if this girl is lying. What's she talking about?" One of the school security guards rushed in, trying to catch whatever they thought was going on.

"Demand he tell you, Coach. Sisi called, and she's stuck. There's no air or anything back there. Make him tell you," I screamed. Trent walked up behind me and said, "I think I know where she is then."

David yelled for Trent to shut up, but Trent kept on talking. "It's the storage room near the basement door."

Coach asked, "How do you know?"

He hesitated for a moment before he said, "Because we used to take girls down there." The coach blew his whistle and said that practice was over. "Call more security, Mr. Brown. David, let's go," he yelled. I jumped at his screaming demand as I watched veins start to surface around his forehead.

"Coach, she's lying. I didn't take Sierra nowhere," David lied again. I looked around and saw the assistant coaches gather the other students in the locker rooms. Most of them were trying to stay to see what was going to happen next.

"I want you to hold him until we get back. Do not let him leave this site," Coach demanded of the security guard. "Let's go, Trent. Show me this room."

The scene outside shocked me as I saw students lined up around the hallway as word obviously got around. The speaker came on and the principal made an announcement demanding students return to their classrooms. I followed the coach and Trent down the flight of stairs leading toward the basement of the school that was shut down. The heat from the summer was seeping through the pipes, making it almost unbearable to breathe. I became even more scared with the thought of Sierra being stuck down here not able to breathe.

"Trent, how much further?" the coach asked, obviously not able to breathe just like myself.

"It's that room right there, sir." He pointed to a dark corner where a broken light blinked off and on. I flipped open my phone calling Sierra's number again, hoping she could get a signal and it would lead us right to her. It went straight to voice mail.

Coach crept to the door and yelled Sierra's name. Nothing. I yelled out. Still nothing.

"Well, maybe she ain't down here like you thought, Cookie," Trent said.

"Coach, aren't you going to open the door and go in?" *I know his big ass ain't scared of the dark.*

He gave me that look that said shut up. I stood there patiently and waited for him to at least touch the doorknob. I was sweating like a beast, and he needed to hurry up. The door made the creepy squeaky sound you hear on scary movies when someone opened a door.

I put myself in the stance that black folks do when they prepare to throw down some punches. Hell, we were in the dark, and I wanted to be prepared.

"Wait! Do you hear that?" It was small whimpers or moaning, but I heard it. I heard feet rushing toward me, and I swung around and screamed out, finding a hiding spot behind Trent.

Trent went into protective mode and yelled out, asking who it was. It was a security guard with a flashlight.

"Great, I'm going to need that," Coach said grabbing the light. We all walked in peddling our feet against the pavement. I stood directly behind Coach, peeking around his body trying to get a visual. Suddenly, I gasped and brought my hand to my mouth.

"Oh man," Trent whispered. The tears were leaving my eyes before I knew it. I quickly ran up to Sierra and proceeded to cover her lower half.

Coach yelled out, "Go call 911!"

"Shhhhh, Sisi, I'm here. I got you." I cradled her in my arms and silently cried, not knowing what else to do but cry. My best friend was laying limp in my arms, and all I wanted to do was seek revenge.

£££

"Cookie, you got a right to be pissed. But revenge is what the devil wants you to do. Now, they got that boy. What you need to do is pray. You think Lyric wasn't able to get passed this. Huh?"

I looked Mama in her face without blinking, my pupils almost fully dilated with rage. Dried up blood stained my clothes and was embedded in my cuticles. Yeah, I was pissed all right. No woman should have to go through this.

"Cookie, I know you can hear me."

21

Cookie

"Let me ask Lyric," I dryly said.

"No. You are gonna leave this be. Leave that alone and let God work it out. You can't change anything he has already written."

"You're right. I need to ask Lyric how she got through it." I could see Lyric's silhouette walk up behind me.

"Mama, it's cool. I'll answer. I felt just like you, Cookie. Mad at the world. Wanting to commit murder. And you know what? I should of proceeded with the case, but I wanted to live my life. You got to see that Sisi will get past this. I still think about it every day, but what didn't kill me made me stronger."

It was sometimes hard to talk to Lyric seriously since I hated her so much. But this very moment was one of those rare occasions when she gave a red cent about my well-being. These moments I liked and although I wanted to hug her and cry in her arms, I knew we weren't that close and it wouldn't feel right. Instead, I got up and nodded my head toward her and Mama and went to my room. I grabbed the first thing I saw off my shelf. My journal.

Days like this I wish I owned a gun. One so big it could blow a whole right through someone's head and you could see straight through it. A graphic thought I know coming from someone like me. But how else am I suppose to feel? Sierra was raped today. The worst part about it, she was raped in Hills, just like Lyric was her freshman year. It's starting to become a damn trend at that school: Rape A Freshman Annual Event. Lyric's rape was one reason why I never trust myself around men. Especially family. Family was the one who tended to do that mess the most. I keep having this reoccurring

22

dream. That I was maybe three or two and someone was touching me there. But I think it's just a dream. But it seemed so real, like maybe it happened but it was so long ago that you don't quite know. My attacker was supposed to be my older cousin. Right on the side of Big Mama's house. Yeah, maybe it was a dream. Hell, who was I to say I could remember something from when I was three.

My thoughts were interrupted when Mama called my name. I placed my pen in between the pages of my journal and walked to my doorway.

"Yes, Mama?"

"Sierra wants to see you. Get dressed. I'll take you to her."

Hips Like Nia Long

"Are you gonna let me drive now?" I asked Lyric.

"Hell, no. The last time I let you behind this wheel you almost hit the curb."

"That was almost three months ago. Surely you have gotten over that."

Baron grabbed my waist and said, "Let's just walk anyhow. It's a nice day. We can catch up. I ain't seen you in a while."

"Are you gonna buy me a new perm when I sweat this one out then?"

He laughed and said, "Yeah, I'll do that."

I looked over to where Lyric, Johnny, Lynn, and Kevin were on the front porch. It was almost six and the summer heat wasn't letting up. I had been hanging out with Lyric more since Sierra decided to spend the summer in Chicago with her dad. The end of my freshman year had come to an end, and I proudly supported my new title of sophomore. Anything to not seem like a child sounded better anyhow.

I took Baron up on his offer to walk to the fajita shack and grab some chicken fajitas and sodas. I waved bye to the group, and we started our hike up Berry Hill, the notorious hill on the south side of Fort Worth. It was fun going down but not going up.

"So, Mr. Baron, you are a high school graduate now. I am so proud of you, boy."

"Hell, yeah, a nigga is certified now. Ain't you proud of your boy?"

24

Smiling from ear to ear I agreed that I was. He had worked so hard to complete his GED assessment, and now he had finished and I wanted him to continue on.

"Man, I can't wait till I can say the same thing. I'm so tired of Hills High that I could scream. And this big-ass hill ain't helping either."

"Well, it's working on them hips," he said, grabbing my waist.

I playfully pushed his hand away and said, "Boy, please, you better look away." He gestured for me to jump on his back so he could carry me, and no way was I going to decline that offer.

"We gonna make this a fun summer, Cook, I promise ya."

Resting my chin on his shoulder I said, "Like what? What you got planned for me?"

"Don't be nosy now. I got you, just know that. I know you had it rough since Sierra left. And I know besides her, I'm your only friend," he teased.

I playfully hit him on his head, "You ain't that special, nigga."

Making it to the top of the hill, I jumped off his back and landed on my feet. "Thanks for the ride." He licked his lips and gave me a weird look.

"What the hell is that?" I laughed at his expression.

"Oh, my bad. I mean, you just shouldn't use words like that."

"What?"

"Ride!"

I punched him in his shoulder and said, "Oh, Baron, come on now. What, you like me now?" I was too busy laughing to see that he wasn't. My laughed stopped, and then my smile faded when I saw his serious face.

25

Cookie

"Wait, I was playing, Baron. What are we talking about here?"

Starting his hike again toward the fajita shack he said, "Nothing. Forget I did that."

"Baron, talk to me. What is it? You seem to always do this. I thought we could talk about anything." He stopped dead in his tracks.

His voice was so high-pitched I could have sworn he was emotional, "That's just it, Cookie, we *don't* talk about everything."

Concern was written all over my face; I brushed his arm and said, "What is it? Tell me."

He struggled with his words for a moment, talking to himself and starting to self-debate. I wasn't a part of it. He looked over and saw Rosedale Park. "Let's go over there and sit."

"This better be good for me to be sitting in this park on this side of Berry." Sitting down on the swings I allowed my feet to make circles in the gravel. "I'm listening."

"A few months back, when we were at Don Carter's I told you that I was cool with you being with ole dude. But I ain't. It seems you're the only person I can talk to. And yeah, I know I am much older, but shit, you don't act like you're fifteen."

"Baron, I see what you mean, but what's your point? I mean, you're nineteen. I couldn't be with you in public, even if I wanted to."

"Then don't. You know me. You know I won't do anything to hurt you. But I would be lying if I said that I'm fine with this. I ain't. I want more. I want you to be my girlfriend."

I had never had anyone tell me this before. In not so many words anyway. To have someone as handsome as Baron look me in my eyes and ask me to be his girlfriend. I mean, no written letter asking me to circle yes, no, or maybe. He straight-out asked me. What was I

26

supposed to say to that? I would be lying if I said I never wanted to kiss him or have him touch me there. Was I a fool at fifteen to try to just be with Carlos? I mean, what was being him with anyhow? I only saw him maybe once a month.

"Baron, are you asking me to be with you? As in, like, in a relationship? Lyric wouldn't even let that happen. She would do anything to make my life miserable. Plus you know I am young. When would we see each other? When you made it to the moon? You don't even have a car." I rambled off at the mouth a mile a minute.

"I'll do what I got to do. But yes, that's what I'm saying, and I don't have to go to the moon to tell you that I want to be with you and I don't want anyone else to be with you."

My mouth went dry. *What the hell did he mean 'be with me'? Doesn't he know that I haven't had sex yet?*

"Baron, I'm a virgin, and I plan to stay that way for a long time. I'm not sure if I want to risk it. We are so close. You sure you want to change this? Change us?"

"If we're friends now, we'll be friends then. Nothing is changing that. But I want to be able to do this too." He got out of his seat and stood before me as I fumbled in the swing. My stomach began to develop those butterflies. They were nearly ripping my stomach into shreds. *Wait! Think of Carlos. Forget that. Have fun, girl.* I played tug-of-war with my emotions as I looked up into Baron's hazel-brown eyes. His honey-brown skin glistened with the summer heat beaming on it. Then I felt that warm sensation in between my legs again. *What IS that feeling?*

Baron leaned down and just looked me in my face for a good ten seconds before I lifted my head brave enough to return the gesture.

27

His lips looked like the softest things I had ever seen. So plump and red and shiny, and it didn't look like a blister ever touched those things.

"Are you gonna kiss me, Baron?" I asked nervously. He went in for the kill. My lips said hello as his said it's about time we met.

Baron brought his arm around my waist and stood me up from the swing, intensifying his kiss. His tongue began to go inside of my mouth, making circles. I moaned as his body heat started to heighten.

"Wait, wait, wait, Baron. Hold up," I managed to say in between pants. "Wait. We're kissing. Oh my God. You just kissed me." I was blushing. I couldn't lie. I felt like I was on cloud nine.

"Yeah, that's what two people do when they like each other, right? Can I do it again?" he teased. I nodded my head and smiled as bright as I could as I walked back into his space, pressing my size C breasts up against his size six-foot-three frame.

Just at that moment, my cell phone buzzed in my pocket, scaring me half to death. Snatching away from my deep, engrossed kiss with Baron, I took out my cell phone to read the name that appeared. Surprisingly at a time like this, it was Carlos.

"It's Carlos," I whispered.

"Oh, that's cool; I'll give you a minute to break the news to him." I raised an eyebrow at Baron. *That is not happening.*

"I'll talk to him later," I said turning the phone completely off and placing it back in my pocket.

"Yeah, you do that. Let's go get these fajitas and tell the rest of the guys about what we've decided."

What you decided, all right. I ain't agreed to nothing. Maybe I'll just let it play out and see how it goes. He's my friend, and what's the worst thing that could happen anyway?

£££

We all hopped in the van and proceeded to head over to Woodlake Apartments to pick up some of Johnny and Baron's friends. Gateway Park was hosting a car show and thousands of Fort Worth natives were destined to be there. Lynn had recently braided my hair back in cornrows, and I would be lying if I said I wasn't looking my best. A sista was looking fine as she could be and looking like I was touching on the age of twenty. Baron kept me close to his side, not letting me breathe.

When we pulled up into the apartments, two guys started to walk out. I almost choked on my soda that I was drinking when I noticed Trent. The world just got smaller. It was rare that I saw anyone from Hills High on this side of town.

"How do y'all know Trent?" I asked before he managed to get closer to the van.

"He's cool with me and Kevin. You know him?" Baron asked scooting us closer to the window to make room for when they got here.

"I go to Hills with him," I said, just before the side door slid open.

"Cookie, what's good, mama?" Trent said, reeking of weed. That's one thing I didn't like was the smell of smoke.

Smiling at a familiar face, I said, "Trent, small world. You hanging with us today?"

He hopped in and said yeah as Lyric started to grin in the driver's seat. It was an obvious tease that she knew I was uncomfortable sitting next to Baron and next to Trent, who obviously liked me. Baron leaned back in his seat and brought his arm around my neck. I rolled my eyes and turned my head toward the window, not

29

really wanting to cater to Baron's ego. We had only been dating now for two weeks and the jealousy was wearing its ugly head right about now.

It only took ten minutes to arrive at Gateway Park, one of the largest parks in Fort Worth. We parked the van across the street and one by one we piled out. Lynn linked with Kevin, Johnny was gripping his black and mild and Lyric's waist, Trent and the other guy were talking about rolling some blunts, and Baron was tirelessly gripping my hand.

"Oh, shit, now, K104 is out here giving out free concert tickets to the Big Mo concert," Lynn yelled out.

"Oh, hell, yeah, let's go see how to get one." Lyric trailed behind Lynn as she sprinted off toward the radio station booth.

"Yo', Lyric, look at who it is," I said, pointing toward Joyclyn Jones, the city's jump-off as they called it.

"Y'all better grip onto your man tight. You know they call her Jo the Ho," Lynn whispered.

"I ain't worried about her. She ain't cute to me anyhow," I said.

"Tell that to the mounts of nigga's she pull with her ass every day. I'm surprised her sister let her hang out with her anyway," Lyric added.

"Who, Dahlia? She is a ho too," Lynn laughed. I rolled my eyes at their continuous gossip when Baron grabbed my hand and led us to the barbecue stand.

Everybody knew I loved hot links and barbecue sauce. I was like a fat kid with a Hershey's bar. I couldn't wait to get that sweet and sour taste in my mouth.

30

"Now, you're getting five cool points with this one," I teased Baron and bit into my hot link and white bread.

"Dang, only five points? What I got to do to get ten?" We laughed. He walked me over toward the bench closest to us that wasn't taken. I looked up and started to take in the scene. About four thousand people were out here. Music blasting from different cars. Food stands selling burgers, tacos, barbecue, and snow cones filled the park. Red paper cups that used to be filled with alcohol now covered the grass.

I took my hot link to my mouth again as Baron said he'd be right back. I watched him step in line to buy some sodas. I couldn't wait because my mouth was burning.

"So that's your man?" Trent said, sitting down beside me.

"You seriously got to lay off the weed, Trent. That's not cute on you."

"Nah, Cookie, please don't start with all that now. I hear it enough at home."

"Okay, whatever. How you been anyway? You ready for your last year in school?"

"Hell, yeah. They talking about a basketball scholarship to UT."

I gave him a love tap on his shoulder and congratulated him. "I'm so happy for you. You lucky, you know that."

"Yeah, you gonna have to be nice to me next year."

"I guess I should since you was there for me and Sierra. I appreciate what you did. You didn't have to."

"I honestly knew David was no good. But rape? That never crossed my mind. Now look at him."

"He's where he deserves to be."

31

"Enough about that," he said placing his cigarette butt in the heel of his shoe. "Show me how you working them Nia Long hips."

Giggling to myself, I said, "I don't know how to dance, Trent; plus Baron will be back soon."

"Oh, come on, he ain't gonna do shit. You a free woman," he said, throwing up his arms, insinuating that the whole world was free.

"Okay, Trent, but don't you touch my booty." I proceeded to ball up my napkin and throw it on the ground. He led me a few feet away as the DJ started a new song by Ludacris that had the crowd going wild. I looked around and noticed cars upon cars that were rebuilt from old rusted metal worth $100,000 now. Some of the cars were custom-painted with loud yellows that hurt my eyes, and some were creamy looking purple. Some of the cars had neon lights inside of them, PlayStations, and all sorts of high-tech gear that I didn't understand.

I tried to focus on rotating my hips into Trent's groin, but I couldn't dance worth a red cent. Soon, I started to bounce with the rhythm that allowed me to look like I was more on beat. I glanced over and saw Lyric and Johnny in a trance.

"Yo', Trent, back the hell up off my girl," I heard Baron's voice as it pierced my ears with rage.

"Hey, Baron, we was just dancing. Cookie and I are cool like that, right?" Trent gestured toward me. I took a deep breath and exhaled out loud, clearly annoyed with the fact that I couldn't have fun.

"Yes, Baron, I have known Trent since sixth grade. It's fine."

"Not the way your ass was on him like that."

I heard Kevin scream out, "Baron, look out." We jumped and turned our head to notice a huge crowd of people running our way.

32

"What's going on?" Trent and I asked at the same time.

"Come on, Cook, let's go! Run!" I felt Baron try to grab my hand, but it slipped through my fingers as I turned around to run away from the stampede that was coming. The screams of the people began to overpower the music as I saw people start to fall to the ground. Thousands of people were headed right toward me.

"Oh, shit! Run, Cookie. Go!" I heard Trent yell, and he grabbed my hand and pulled me in the direction of where we had parked.

"Run, Lyric, go, go!" I screamed out. It was if at that moment nothing was around us as our eyes met. I saw the fear in hers as she saw mine. Our stare-down was snatched away as I saw Johnny pull her arm to start running. Just like that, everything went back into play.

"Cookie!" I heard Baron scream. He was a couple feet in front of me. I saw something in his eyes as he glanced back to see where I was. I tightened my grip onto Trent. I felt he was my only savior at this moment, allowing me to know that I was not alone in this nightmare.

All of a sudden I felt a huge sting. I screamed out in pain as Trent's hands loosened. I heard him scream out in agony. I heard the stomping of everyone's feet coming toward us and somehow I still heard Baron's voice yelling for me.

As if I were electrocuted, my body jerked from the loud blast.

Then again. *Bam!*

Bam!

Bam!

I heard it three more times as I saw Trent fall to the ground. I screamed out, my voice hitting a note that you hear those professional opera singers sing. I squeezed his hand and yelled for him to come on and get up. A stampede of girls ran toward us, knocking me to the ground. I fell face forward on top of Trent. Next, I felt sharp pains from people's feet start to trample over my body. I slightly raised my head and screamed Trent's name again.

His face was toward me, and I could see blood drizzle out of his mouth. His head was trembling. "What's wrong, Trent? Get up. Come on," I managed to say in between the sharp pains that were shooting through my body.

"Go, Cookie. Go," he whispered. I looked over and noticed his back was wet. I brushed my hand over it, and it was warm. I put my arm around his waist and told him again to come on.

I could hear Baron's voice closer. He was telling people to watch out.

I saw a tear fall from Trent's eyes. "Trent!" I screamed again, shaking him like a rag doll. I was now hysterical with the tears that were burning my eyes. I looked at my hand and noticed it was blood.

Wait a minute. Those were gunshots. Oh my God, is Trent shot? What is this?

Trent cried out, "It hurts." He started to cough uncontrollably. I leaned in closer, my nose to his nose and said, "I got you. It's okay. Just try to get up. Please."

I begged him. I cried out for him to come on over and over until I saw him stare me in the eyes. He was telling me something, but he didn't say anything.

"I'm here," I whispered to him again. "Trent, can you hear me? I'm here; come on." Then I noticed he was still. His eyes went dark. There were no more tears.

34

I screamed out like I used to in church. When the Holy Ghost came upon you and all you wanted to do was scream, shout, and cry out. There was a pain all through my body, but my chest ached the most. I screamed and shook Trent to wake up. His eyes were open, but there was no life in them. I had never seen someone's eyes go so dark and vacant.

"Cookie, I got you. Come on, I got you. It's okay." Baron ripped me up by my arms and threw me over his shoulders. I kept reaching out for Trent, screaming that I couldn't leave him. I yelled for Baron to go back.

I heard another blast and in my mind, that was it. I just knew that I was dead too.

What Is Life For Anyway?

I didn't notice that tears were coming from my eyes. I didn't notice the sadness in my heart as I made my way to my first-period class. Sophomore year had started and somewhere deep down I just wanted to die. Classmates kept saying to each other, *did you hear what happened to Trent?* I wanted to scream out, *Yes! He died in my arms, now leave me alone.*

"I'm not going to ask you if you're okay, Cookie. Because I know you're not. But we will get through this together. It's hard for me to be back here too. But I am here, so we can get through this together," Sierra said taking my hand in hers.

I hurried and wiped away the tears that left my eyes and gave her a weak smile. "I'll be okay. What about you? First day of school means all new territory."

"After last year, I'm going to focus more on school. You should too and leave Baron alone. He's too old for you anyway."

"This is why I just wanted to stay friends with him. But he gets me. More than Carlos anyhow."

"Speaking of Carlos, did you tell him what happened?"

"No. I haven't talked to him all summer while you were gone."

"What? Why, Cook? That is serious."

"What was the point? I hadn't seen him, or you, for that matter, all summer. To top shit off, I spent three weeks of that in the house healing all those damn wounds. But who is going to heal the one

36

that haunts me in my dreams every night? I mean, it was Trent. Why did this have to happen?" I said, slamming my locker door in anger.

"Okay, Cookie, you don't want the whole school to know what went down and start this whole school gossip. I know you're still hurt. But pray. What happened to you doing that?"

"Prayer left my life when Higher Touch left. Fuck that," I said in anger and walked off. I couldn't believe what I just said, but that was another wound I got from my church, Higher Touch, disbanding like it did.

£££

The usual scene at Higher Touch Fellowship Worship Center was chairs thrown every which way, hands raised, mouths screaming and repenting of their daily sins, and people shouting and dancing in the Holy Ghost. We always knew when the church was about to break down into its usual shout and praise, which is why most of our services lasted five hours instead of the normal two to three hours.

Our favorite section was to sit directly by the front door. Mama would sit in the back row near the usher stand, and Lyric and I would be about two or three rows in front. When Bishop came in, the whole church would stand to welcome him. That was about three hundred folks that squeezed their way in the one-flat story building. Ninety-five percent of the congregation was black with a few sprinkles of whites and Hispanics.

I loved Sunday mornings, and by the time I was eleven, Lola and Jayla had moved out of the house and to Corpus Christi, which meant we didn't go to church anymore every day of the week. So Sundays was the day I scanned the room for potential eye candy. Other than Carlos, that is, back then. Lynn was active in the church, singing in the choir. Her voice was one of the most beautiful tones I had heard back then. Unlike Lyric and I, who couldn't sing a note on-key.

It wasn't easy liking the pastor's stepson, but I guess the thrill made it all worth it. I liked when Mama bought me a new dress that tended to show off my young curves. I would get up to go to the bathroom, holding up one finger which was a church rule for respect, just to show off my outfit sometimes.

One thing I did hate though about sitting in the same row with Mama, when we sat with her, was you could be deep in thought about whatever it was Bishop was preaching about and suddenly become consumed with this horrible odor. I remember one time when I was in one of my sleepy spells, I was slapped out of my trance by an unbearable stench. I jerked up and looked toward Lyric, who had already started to laugh uncontrollably. I eyed her, and she eyed me back as we read each other's weekly signals that Mama had yet again let a nasty fart out.

Not just any fart at that. These ones you felt an animal died or a stink bomb was let loose and it was time to duck for cover. I turned around toward Mama to give her the evil eye because right about now my stomach was hurting from the stench.

"Shhhhh, shut up, Cookie," is what she normally said before I had any chance to complain.

I would bow my head in my lap and laugh, wondering if everyone else in the section smelled this godforsaken stench. Sometimes I couldn't hold my laughter in. I'd have to walk outside the church door to relieve the scream that was stuck in my throat, threatening to erupt.

Times like this made church fun but yet unbearable. When Bishop would get deep into his sermon, he would preach and there was never a Sunday when his suit didn't stain with sweat. Not just any ole sweat. The kind that made your shirt completely wet when he hugged you good-bye. I would sometimes find myself sitting in the back of the church after service, waiting for Bishop to be done giving everyone a farewell at the front door. It would take maybe an hour to dry after his wet hug.

But one thing for sure, Mama loved to go to church. She read her Bible daily, quoted scriptures every hour on the hour, and at the same time, could cuss you out a good one. When the sermon got good, Mama would raise up her handkerchief and scream out, "Yeah!" or "Do it, God!" Her yells were so loud that the entire section jumped in shock at her heavy tone. And Mama's tone was *very* heavy. She could give Barry White a run for his money. I used to love to see her jump out of her seat, raise up her skirt, run up to the front of the podium where Bishop stood, and throw her handkerchief at him in approval.

I used to giggle into my hand and bashfully hide my face when she did stuff like that. But for the members of Higher Touch, that was the highlight of the service. Sister Della is what they called her.

I had to get used to sharing my mother with others who needed advice or guidance. She seemed to be everyone's mama. After church, we would go home, eat chicken, and call it a night. We used to head back to night service, but that tradition soon faded once the congregation started too.

Maybe everyone started to leave once Bishop divorced his wife. It was more of a hypercritical move. But it seemed to take a toll on the church. I remember one Sunday Bishop addressed the church after months of gossip and rumors about people wanting to leave because others were. "Stand up if at some point you felt like leaving the church," he said one Sunday, and my mind was blown when more than ninety percent of the people stood. That day was a wake-up call because even Mama stood.

He asked for us to pray and stick together, but within less than a year, the three hundred-plus people who called Higher Touch home had dropped to a measly fifty. By this time, Carlos and his mama were long gone, and with Lyric being eighteen now, she started going to Lynn's new church. I had to beg Mama to leave too, and right before I entered high school, we finally left to find a new church home. The family I had known since I was three had now disappeared and was a faded memory. With them gone, my faith weakened.

£££

I was glad when the first day of school ended. There was a memorial in the school chow hall with a huge photo of Trent surrounded by candles and flowers. Some of the teammates had put his jersey there and wrote a letter.

"If it wasn't for you, Trent, they wouldn't have found me so quick. Thank you and rest in peace," I heard Sierra whisper to his photo.

"I can't do this, Sierra, let's go." We walked out to the front of the school to wait on Mama to come pick us up when I noticed a familiar face.

"What is Carlos doing here?"

Sierra gave me that "I'm guilty" look. I rolled my eyes and let out an aggravated sigh.

He hopped out of his car and ran up to me, not letting me even extend my arms as he held me tightly. Without warning, tears started to burst out of my eyes as I began to weep into his arms. "Get me out of here," I muffled a scream in between sobs. I felt Sierra grab my backpack as we walked to his car and hopped in.

"I wish you would have called me, Cookie," Carlos said as we drove off.

Staring out the window, I tried to ignore him. We pulled up in front of Sierra's house, and she said she would call me later. I gave her a weak smile and nodded my head that I understood.

Noticing that our trail was not leading to my house I said, "Where the hell are we going?"

"What? Are you mad at me, Cookie?"

I rolled my eyes and folded my arms, clearly aggravated. "Take me home, Carlos."

"No, that's okay. I'll pass on that. I told Mama I'll have you there in an hour."

Angrily turning toward him I said, "What you got to say now? Huh? You ain't too worried about little ole me until you found out I almost died. Ain't that a bitch?"

"Damn, Cook, when did you start talking like that? I do care about you. Regardless if you think so or not. You should know that right about now."

"Funny thing is I don't. I ain't seen you since we was at the lake. This is some bull, and you know it. Why are you here now? Honestly tell me."

Stuttering he said, "I heard what happened." He pulled over to the park where our church once held a youth event. It brought back unwanted memories.

"Yeah, I thought so. That's the only reason. I think it's good for us to be apart. That night made me realize life is so short. What you think, all I did was wait around for you all summer?" I smirked.

"What does that mean?"

"What, you want me to do a recap? I was shot at. I watched my friend die in my arms, only to be bedridden for three weeks, with only his memory to haunt me. Not a phone call or a visit from you. The only reason I was there at that park was to be with someone who cared enough about me. Someone who still calls me every day to check up on me. But not you. You, Carlos, are a joke. One, I choose, to not wallow in."

"Oh, you're saying you seeing somebody else?"

"You ain't asked me to be your girl, nor am I willing to be just with one person anyhow. I just turned fifteen, by the way. Had you known that, you might have sent a gift."

"Cookie, I know you're pissed at me, but I do care. I do take you for granted, but I try to make everybody happy."

"Carlos, take me home please. I need to rest. Today wasn't a good day."

"I will, but I ain't leaving your sight. Trust me."

Tamika Newhouse

When A Girl Becomes A Woman

The smell started to become all too familiar as I took it in between my index finger and my thumb and brought it to my lips. It had a sweet scent to it. It wasn't all too bad once you smoked it. I took a long drag of its ingredients and allowed the smoke to sit in my lungs for a few seconds before I let out an exhale. I formed my lips in an O as I made smokey o's.

"Can you pass, please, Ms. I Am Grown Now?" Lyric said as I tried to concentrate on the weed's affect.

"Here, and don't wet the butt, please. I don't want to feel like I'm kissing Johnny." We all laughed in unison. Baron had walked back outside on the back porch and had laid the wings we ordered in the middle of the table. I leaned back in my seat after grabbing two.

I glanced over and noticed Kevin and Lynn engrossed in a deep-throat kiss. Noticing Baron on my left, I scooted over in my seat to allow him to sit next to me.

"When is Lyric passing?" Baron asked agitated.

I joked and said, "Johnny, how are you going to sell and smoke weed? Them Hispanics going to come looking for you like they did Smokey in *Friday*." We all laughed uncontrollably as the affects of the weed made us looser than usual.

"Girl, I can handle mine. Look at you thinking you all bad and shit," Johnny said as I took the weed from his fingers to pass to Baron.

"Yummm, these wings are off the hook. Baron, please tell your mama to order some more," I asked. He hopped up and did just

44

that. His mama was a young woman that didn't care what we did, and that was just fine by us.

It had been six months since my tragic episode with Trent and the shooting. I was on the end of my sophomore year, and I had a new look on life. I started to care less about being perfect and more about just staying in the moment.

"We'll be back," Johnny said, grabbing Lyric's hand.

"Where y'all going?" Lynn asked. She stood up and told Kevin to follow. They proceeded to tell them that they were headed to the west side to get some more weed.

"Don't get that smell in Mama's van. Roll with the windows down," I said before they all left.

"So, Cookie, we get to be alone," Baron boasted.

I giggled at his obvious excitement and said, "Yes, indeed. What do you want to do?"

He leaned toward me and went in for the kill as he proceeded to kiss me again. My mind was going a mile a minute as I enjoyed the warm sensations shoot through my body.

"Let's go inside," I said in between a kiss.

"OK." He took me by the hand and led me to his room which was adjacent to the backyard patio door. A huge convenience.

I plopped down on the bed and lay my head down on his pillow as he lay beside me, and I nuzzled my nose into his neck, enjoying the safe feeling I felt when I was with him.

"I just love being with you," he whispered.

"Me too. More when we're alone. It seems no one ever lets us be. Moments like these are so rare."

I lifted my head and allowed his lips to find mine and fell into a trance. His hand started to rub all over my waist down to my hips, and he squeezed my butt. I just wanted this warm pulsating feeling in between my legs to be taken care of. I didn't know what it exactly meant, but I knew I just wanted to have sex for whatever reason.

I moaned in between my pecks and licks, letting him know I enjoyed this feeling. I pressed my C cups on his chiseled chest and wrap my legs around him. He was now placed right in the middle of my embrace as our kisses intensified with heat and passion.

He brought his hands under my skirt and brought his fingers to my nectar. I hadn't had a boy finger me since the one time I let this boy do it my freshman year. That was the last time I allowed myself to get that vulnerable. But Baron was different. I've known him for almost a year now, and he felt safe. This is why I didn't protest when I felt him maneuver my panties all the way down to my feet.

I widened my legs as he inserted his fingers, jabbing them in and out. "Hmmm, Cookie, you feel so good, baby."

I blushed at his acceptance that he liked what he felt as I felt him pull his shorts downward. I was anticipating his touch down there. I heard the stories of your first time being horrible. That the pain was unbearable and that your skin broke so badly that you bled like a gutted fish.

When I felt something pointy I figured he was still using his finger; that is, until the feeling started to not feel good and started to hurt. I moaned in agony.

"Shhh, baby, I got you," he whispered.

I lay there as he inserted more of what I came to know was not his finger. It was harder than a finger, and it was larger than a finger,

46

and then the pain started to intensify. I started to moan out louder in agony, so he brought his hand and covered my mouth so that my yells weren't heard.

"It's okay, baby. You feel so good," he said in between huffs and puff. Suddenly, I felt like a knife entered my abdomen. By now, the pain was excruciating. Surprisingly, I didn't cry, and the pain started to even out. Three minutes felt like twenty as Baron's rhythm started to subside and slow down.

"Whew, that was good, baby."

"Yeah, for you," I said in a muffled voice. My mouth was dry, and I was in need of a cold towel to place on my hot, sore vagina. He switched on the light, and I could have sworn a pound of blood covered his sheets.

"Oh, shit, let's get this cleaned up before everybody gets back here," he said.

I followed his lead by hurrying to the bathroom and running some cold water. He came in five minutes behind me and said, "Wow, Cookie, you wasn't lying about being a virgin. I wish it could have been more special."

Feeling like I was walking bowlegged I said, "Yeah, maybe next time it'll be better."

"Oh, next time, huh?" He smiled from ear to ear.

I threw a towel at him and said, "Don't push your luck." We washed off and for the first time I saw a grown man naked. I swallowed hard as I tried not to stare but was very curious to see just what had been inside of me. I tell you, it wasn't cute at all. More like an ugly, hairy snake that needed some tanning.

47

As we made our way back through his room, I noticed he changed his sheets. I knew those sheets were gonna be thrown away. We sat back on the porch and grabbed some more wings. Now I sat down slower than usual as my vagina hurt.

"You know I love you, Cookie."

I almost choked on my hot wing when I snatched my head to look at Baron. "Love?"

"Yeah, you don't have to say it back, but I'm going to college just because you told me too. I realized that I do love you, and this night is only the beginning."

I smiled just a little, not really knowing what to say to that. I mean, what was love anyhow? I know Baron was almost twenty but at barely sixteen, I didn't know what love was.

"You know I care about you too, Baron. And when I feel the same about you, I'll make sure you're the first to know." I bit into my wing as he nodded that he understood. We leaned back in the swing and looked at the dark sky, talking about the future and his plans for college.

I was so happy for him and that he was perusing something so much better.

£££

It had been two weeks since I lost my virginity, and in those two weeks I had sex with Baron two more times. The third time felt like a roller coaster that I wanted to stay on forever. I was at Sierra's house replaying the episodes in my head.

"So you a woman now?" she asked.

"Yes, ma'am. Not only that, it's only with one guy."

"Yeah ... for now. You and Carlos seem to be joined at the hip now."

I laughed out and blushed because her statement was true. "Is it possible to like two guys at the same time?"

"Yeah, I guess. You know I haven't been that interested in boys since ... you know ... the incident. But this new guy who is at my church, he is just so dreamy." Sierra went into space with her thoughts as her smile broadened.

"Wow, I'm going to have to meet this mystery guy. He sounds like a good one."

"He is. We've been talking on the phone, but it hasn't been sexually based or anything. I think you should meet him."

"You know, we should all just set a date because we haven't done it in a while. I miss hanging out."

"Girl, please. You seem to always be with Lyric and the crew. Does Lyric know you gave it up to Baron?"

"She ain't stupid. I guess she don't care as long as it ain't with Carlos. She would do anything to control something, and Mama ain't letting me date yet, so I can't see him when I want to. The only time I can have fun is when I'm with Lynn and Lyric."

"I know you be missing him. Call him. Tonight let's go hang out with him and Sean, my new boo. You can tell your mama you with me and my sister, and I can tell Mama that we are being dropped off at the bowling alley by Lyric. Cool?"

I excitedly picked up the phone and dialed Carlos's number. "Hey, are you busy?"

"I'm never to busy for you."

"Well ..." I teased.

49

"Oh, you gonna play me like that?" he joked.

"Are you busy tonight? It's the weekend, and I wanted to hang out with you. I won't be going with Lyric this weekend. I just wanted to finally spend some time with you."

"Now you know I'm up for it. If I had plans I'd cancel them anyway to spend time with my girl. I'll be there in two hours. Don't be looking too fine to where I got to fight a nigga."

I laughed and said, "I'll see you then." Sierra called Sean, and he said he was going to meet up with us at Chili's, a local restaurant. I wanted to go on what seemed like a date with Carlos. I know dating a younger girl was getting annoying since I couldn't do much.

But I was so anxious to have this date with him. I made sure to dress warm in some tight-fitted jeans and knee-high boots so the winter frost wouldn't spoil my mood.

"You look cute, girl," Sierra said, examining my outfit. We heard the horn blow outside and grabbed our purses and ran out to Sierra's sister's car.

Arriving at Chili's, we sat in the waiting area until Sierra spotted Sean. He was pretty cute and the total opposite of her normal taste in guys. He seemed better mannered, and the fact that he was a Christian boy was apparent in his demeanor. It was a good change for Sierra.

By the time fifteen more minutes passed by, I flipped open my phone to call Carlos and see what was taking him so long. But he didn't answer. By the time another twenty minutes rolled by, I knew he wasn't coming.

"Y'all, just go eat. We've been sitting here for an hour, Sierra."

"Cookie, you sure?"

"Yeah, I don't want to ruin y'all date. I'll just have Lyric come and get me because obviously Carlos is standing me up."

Sierra nodded her head toward me and Sean and she walked over to the receptionist to be seated. I pulled out my cell phone and called Lyric. Surprisingly, she agreed to come and get me. I walked over to the bar to get me an order to go, and by time that was ready, my phone buzzed in my hand. Lyric was outside.

After telling Sierra bye, I walked outside and noticed Lyric had the van full of people. My pace sped up as I saw Baron slid open the door. My boo was here.

"Hey, Baron," I said wrapping my arms around his neck.

"Ugh, get your fast tail in the car," Lynn joked.

I noticed that the van held one other female I didn't know and three guys. Some I had seen from around the way.

"Cook, what was you doing up here?" Lyric asked.

"Hanging with Sierra but got bored 'cause her boyfriend showed up. What we getting into tonight?"

Baron kissed me on the cheek and said, "We heading into Eastwood for this house party. I been asking where you were since they picked me up."

"You missed me, huh?" I teased. We got on the freeway heading to the party Baron had mentioned. This would be one of the many parties I would witness.

Money Grows On Trees

"OK, now, remember, don't get caught. If you see a worker coming, just run your ass out of there. But whatever you do, don't take the clothes to the dressing room. They are looking for folks to steal back there. You got to take it off the floor," Lyric informed me.

"Oh, I got this. I take my baby's stroller in all the time and just drop the clothes in there," Kyra said. I leaned forward in the backseat and pressed my head up against the driver's seat to listen better. I was taking mental notes like we were about to go rob a bank.

"OK, Lynn and I will go in first. Then, Cook, you and Kyra follow in five minutes. We in and out in ten minutes. When you get your shit, just leave. Don't worry about nobody else."

"How many times have y'all done this?" I asked, wondering how long they been acting like the ladies in *Set It Off*.

"Enough times to know that if you get caught you on your own," Lyric said. "And, Cook, you better not get caught, because if you do, Mama is going to beat my ass."

"I got this. I'm ready. Let's go." I watched Lynn and Lyric walk into Old Navy as if they were casual customers looking to shop. Out of all the stores to steal from these days it was Old Navy that had very little to no security.

I turned to look at Kyra pull the baby carrier out of the trunk and place her baby in it. She nodded toward me, and I hopped out of the van and followed suit. I told myself to act natural; I can do this.

Inside, I walked toward the teen girls section looking for the size eights. My size. I hadn't stolen any clothes before, but after seeing

Lynn come home with new stuff all the time I felt it was time for me to learn the ropes. Now here I was, strolling the aisle looking for what I wanted to take.

I noticed a denim shirt and short set that would look good on my figure. It looked like the shirt would show just above my navel. I walked over toward the rack and pretended to be interested. I made sure there was no space between me and the clothes rack. I pulled my purse around to sit directly in front of my stomach and began to fumble with the hanger. The shorts slipped off. I bundled it up and stuffed it in my purse. I did the same to the shirt.

I looked over the rack after I had achieved my heist and noticed Kyra nose deep in stuffing baby clothes in the stroller. I looked around to see if anyone was coming. The coast was clear.

I signaled for her to hurry up. I had what I wanted. I turned around suddenly to walk out of the store when I bumped directly into a worker.

"Oh, sorry," I said coolly.

"No problem," the person replied and talked into his walkie-talkie as he proceeded to walk back toward where I just left. I could feel my heart beating in my throat. I put some speed in my step and walked toward the front entrance.

"Ma'am, did you find anything today?"

Shit, I'm caught.

"No, maybe next time," I said with a hint of nervousness in my voice. Did she know I had stolen clothes in my purse? How? I was careful and made sure no one saw me. I looked over her and saw Lynn walk out the front door. *Well, they did say I was on my own.*

"Well, hopefully, next time," the worker said. "Have a great day."

I breathed a sigh of relief and walked past her and the afternoon breeze hit me. I felt like I was breathing freedom for the first time in years.

Making it to the van Lynn said, "I thought you were caught."

I looked behind me and saw Lyric and Kyra walking toward us. "No, I made it out all right and got me an outfit."

"Just one?" Lyric asked. Her purse was obviously stuffed. I nodded my head yeah. It wasn't like I was a pro at this and did it every day. We threw our bags in the back and hopped in the van and drove off.

This would be one of the many heists I would be a part of, and it started to become like second nature.

£££

"I want you to take this to school with you, Cookie, and see if anyone is willing to cash them. Doesn't matter who, but they got to give us $300 off the profit, cool?"

Looking at the blank checks I said, "Where did you get these from?"

"Johnny hooked us up. He's selling them to everybody."

"We've upgraded from heisting the stores, huh?" I laughed and took a few of the checks, stuffing them into my backpack. "I think I know a few who will want some of these. I'll let you know." The new scheme on our agenda was selling stolen checks. It didn't matter where the source came from as long as in the end we got money. I knew it was wrong, but at the same time, I didn't care.

Hoping out of the van, I walked up to the front doors of Hills to start my day. I made certain to wear the new clothes I had stolen from our latest heist. Folks started to take notice of my new expensive gear. I was looking better than most of my classmates from my new Polo purse, to the Nautica jeans which I made sure were extra tight around my hips, to the new Chanel perfume I made sure to spray in between my breasts and both sides of my neck. I was looking real fly.

Popping my new cherry lip gloss on my lips, I passed a crowd of seniors and heard one say, "Yo', Cookie, bring your fine ass here."

I glanced over stopping my stroll to first period and said, "You need to come better than that if you're talking to me."

Out of the crowd, Ken walked out and said, "I forgot your ass is all mean and shit." Wrapping his arm around my shoulder he leaned in and said, "So when are you going to stop fronting and let me take you out?"

"Ken, why must you come up to me like one of these random sophomores around here? You wanna take me out, huh?" I smiled, sucking on my bottom lip.

"Hell, yeah, let me take you out." Ken was at least six foot tall, had a chocolate complexion like me, and he always kept himself looking clean.

"Give me your number; perhaps I can think about it."

Laughing, he said, "Aw, come on, man, are you for real?"

"Give me your number, Ken. Why can't a girl ask for your number instead?"

Pulling out a piece of paper from his backpack he asked, "Are you going to call me?"

"Sure." I took his number in my hand and walked into Mrs. Thompson's classroom for first period. I loved the attention, and guys loved girls they couldn't have.

It wasn't long into the day that I had already solicited three of my classmates who were interested in the blank checks Lyric gave me. I told them I needed $300 up front because I wasn't risking them never giving me any money. It was easy money and quick cash for sure.

I planned on giving Lyric half of the $300 since I had made the initial connect and would put the other half up toward something for Mama. I knew down the line she would need some money on bills.

Walking out of my last period I noticed a familiar face and a smile creeped up across my face. I quickly let it disappear so that he wouldn't know I was happy to see him.

"Hey, beautiful."

I asked, "What are you doing here?" Not forgetting that he stood me up and didn't offer any explanation.

"I came to give you and Sierra a ride home and maybe grab something to eat."

Rolling my eyes, I said, "Sierra isn't at school today, and I would rather walk the five miles home."

I pushed past him and walked out of the school doors, making sure not to look back at him. Maybe I was overreacting, but truth be told, I was tired of him popping in and out. Enough was enough.

£££

Tap, tap!

I jumped up in my bed looking around and noticed no one was there. My bedroom door was closed shut, and my fan was on full blast.

Other than the house cracks, I couldn't hear or see a damn thing. But then again I heard the tapping.

Tap, tap!

I looked toward my window and peeked through one of my blinds. *What in the world is Carlos doing at my window?* I wondered if Lyric could hear the tapping too with her window being almost adjacent to mine.

Unlocking my window I slid it up halfway and said, "What are you doing here? It's the middle of the night." I looked over his shoulder and saw his Monte Carlo parked directly in front of our house. If Mama saw this I just knew she was going to kill me.

"Baby, please let me talk to you."

Agitated and scared at the same moment with Mama right across the hallway, I said, "What time is it?"

"It's a little after one a.m."

"This better be good then." He looked down and smiled at me and I looked down to notice I was just in a T-shirt and panties. I hit him on the shoulder and said, "Eyes up front, mister."

Laughing, he signaled for me to lean in for a kiss. My body temperature instantly rose as I stretched my head out of the window to place my full lips on his. Moaning in between our deep kisses he asked, "What if I come in and lay down with you for a minute?"

"Boy, don't you know Mama would kill you? What's a minute?"

"Cookie, please, I miss you, and I just want to feel you next to me. Mama won't even know." I started to mentally debate his question. He was right. Mama would more likely never know because she rarely came into my room.

57

"If you promise to be a good boy, I'll let you come inside."

Smiling, he whispered, "I promise." I leaned back raising the window all the way for him to climb in. All I kept thinking was what if one of these noisy-ass white neighbors would see Carlos and tell on me.

In my bed, he took his hand and wrapped it around my waist. It didn't take long to notice that this hand trailed just above my butt where my panties were. I didn't feel self-conscious about being half-naked. After all, Baron had taught me more than a few things.

He whispered, "You know we have never been this close and alone before."

I smiled and said, "Lyric is in the next room, and Mama is on the other side of this door. We are definitely not alone."

"I mean like this, Cook, having you in my arms. I could get used to this."

"So what did you want to talk to me about?"

"I'm sorry for standing you up the other day. I have been going through some things with my mama, and my sister is coming back home with all of her kids."

"She's getting a divorce?"

"Yea, and I ain't trying to be around all that drama. I may move out."

"You got a year left in school. Where you going to move to?"

"I'm thinking of sharing an apartment with some of my friends. It'll be good for me to concentrate and graduate and finally get out of here." I cringed at his declaration of leaving Fort Worth.

"You're trying to leave?" I didn't want to sound selfish or upset, but I had practically loved this boy since I was twelve. I couldn't imagine him gone.

He looked down at me and adjusted how we lay so that the moonlight beamed across my face, "Cookie, I'm not going to leave you, but I don't know what I am going to do. You know I love you, right?"

It was if my heart skipped a rhythm, and the air left my lungs. In all the years that I had known him, he has never said those words to me. And for the first time in my life, those words made me want to cry. It was as if I got stabbed at this very moment I wouldn't feel a thing. His words made me feel invincible and powerful.

My mouth was dry as I repeated his statement. "You love me?"

"You know I do. Shit, don't nobody else matter but you." He looked me directly in my eyes, and I bashfully looked away, making his neck my new focus.

He brought his hand to my chin, raising my face up to meet his again. Leaning forward, he took his lips and rubbed them across mine. I moaned as my body heat started to rise. I knew this feeling like the back of my hand now. I was getting aroused by his touch. I wanted to feel him inside of me as I had done with Baron. *But how do I tell him that?*

My moaning escalated as his tongue entered in my mouth. "Carlos," I whispered in between our kisses. He answered with a moan. "I want to feel you tonight."

I opened my legs and motioned for him to touch me there. "You want to have sex, Cook?" he quizzed me. I read his expression and could tell that he was excited but surprised at the same time.

"Yes, I'm ready."

He leaned back in to kiss me, pressing his body against mine, and I could feel his hardness grow. Leaning back on my side of the bed I spread my legs even more, allowing him to gain easier access.

I had always imagined that my first time would be with someone like Carlos, but remembering the pain of my first time, I was glad that he wasn't. I wanted this time to be special. I wanted to enjoy the feeling of our bodies connecting.

My anticipation caused my left leg to shake uncontrollably. I felt his hands reach my panties as he slid them down. I was soon as bare as the day I was born, and I closed my eyes and allowed my body, mind, and spirit to connect with Carlos in more ways than one. I had to be honest. I loved this boy.

Tamika Newhouse

Party Like A Rock Star

Mama's big white van was full of folks, and I had managed to convince Lyric to let Sierra come out and hang with us. It was Sunday night, and although I had school in the morning, Mama never gave me a curfew if I was with Lyric. Thinking back now, she should have.

The back row was full of some of Lynn and Kyra's friends. We opted out to hanging out with Kevin, Baron, and Johnny tonight because on Sundays, everyone and they mama was out in EastWood. Miller Street was the central location. Talk about hundreds of cars in the street blasting music and dancing and drinking. It was a true block party. I loved Sunday nights.

"Yo', let me out here, Lyric. I'm gonna get some cigars," one of Lynn's friends said.

Lyric parked the car in the parking lot of a fast-food place, and one-by-one, we piled out.

"Wow, Cookie, look at all of these folks," Sierra said. Her eyes were out of her head as she took in the crowd. This was my peoples, the ones who truly represented "Funkytown" Fort Worth. "Have you been out here before with all these folks?"

"Yep, sure have. It's off the hook, ain't it?" I laughed, taking one of the liquor coolers into my hand and popping it open. "You want one, Sierra?" She looked at me with uncertainty, and then took the drink in her hand.

The parking lot we were in held at least 30 other cars. Folks of all ages were jamming to K104, and some others were playing the latest underground music. Artists that no other state knew, like Z-RO, Big

Moe, Mike Jones, DJ Screw, Lil' Flip, Big Hawk, Tela, Magnificent, ESG, and Fat Pat were blaring through everyone's systems. These artists would all soon be famous though.

"Hey, Cookie, somebody is calling my phone for you," I heard Lyric call out. She stood on the opposite side of the van talking to a guy who wanted to get her number. Reaching for the phone I put it to my ear.

"Hey, who is this?"

"Hey, Cook, where are y'all at tonight?"

Smiling and instantly recognizing Carlos's voice I said, "Right now, we are on Miller, and then we're going to head over to Arlington Lake for the block party there."

"You kind of young to be out there with all those folks, Cook. Why don't I come pick you up and we go hang?" I rolled my eyes in annoyance.

"Hey, what's your name?" I looked over and saw one of the finest guys I had seen in a long time. Resembling the singer Usher, I give him my brightest smile and said hello. Carlos, hearing his voice in the background, angrily started to interrogate me.

"Who are you out with, Cookie? That doesn't sound like Lyric or Sierra."

"Hey, Carlos, let me call you back, OK? I'm hanging out with my friends tonight." Before he could protest, I flipped the phone shut and gave Mr. New Guy my full attention.

"So what's your name?" he asked.

"You can call me Cookie." I made sure to pop my full lips and bash my eyes just a tad more than usual. He was too cute for me to not to get his number. "Give me one minute," I said, walking back to Lyric and handing her the phone. "If Carlos calls back, don't answer."

Laughing, she said, "Oh, so you're a player now. I got you."

I didn't want to view myself as a young girl playing the field, and I did love him, but I was going to have fun too. I walked back over to the mystery guy and resumed my conversation.

"I'm not going to hold you long, Cookie, right? I just wanted to know if I could have your number."

"What's your name?"

"Denzel." I stopped dead in my tracks and wanted to scream out in laughter. How in the world was his name attached to such a fine specimen and he is a fine specimen himself?

Trying to cover up my laugh I said, "Well, Denzel, you can give me your number, and I'll call you." He laughed off my gesture and asked me for a pen and paper. I jotted it down and told him I'd call him later tonight.

"I see you wasted no time getting a few numbers," Sierra laughed. She was looser than usual.

"Sierra, I know you haven't been over here drinking up all the alcohol, girl. Slow down."

"No, I only had one."

"You tipsy off of one drink? OK, girl, I got to get you out more often." I picked up my drink and took another swallow. Then I looked up and noticed a crowd of folks rush over to a car.

"Yo', something is going down," I heard Lynn scream.

Of course something is going down; this is Fort Worth and its hundreds of black folks in one spot.

"Oh my goodness, look at that girl on top of that car."

64

My mouth dropped in shock as I saw a girl standing on top of a truck dancing like she was on a stripper pole. Her breasts and ass were exposed and she looked damn near the same age as me.

"Do she think that's cute, letting niggas look at her poo nanny for free?" Lyric yelled out.

"They are rocking the mess out of that car; she's going to start a riot," I added. The scene was scary in more ways than once. There were at least fifty men surrounding that truck trying to reach up and grab anything that was connected to her body. When she noticed the ever-growing crowd, I saw the fear and regret on her face.

"Now look at her. She scared now," Lynn said.

"This is horrible. Who's going to help her?" Sierra added.

I stood there scared for her and what those men might do, but what genius would strip in public? I turned my head when I saw the flashing lights and suddenly the roar of footsteps made the ground shake.

"Five-O is coming. Y'all load up. Let's go," I heard one of Kyra's friends say.

"Is that the police? Why are we running? What's going on?" Sierra asked. I forgot she had never been out with us before.

"Sierra, gets your Mary Poppins ass in the car before we all get arrested," Lynn yelled. I gave Sierra a push to get in so everyone else could climb in. You could barely hear yourself breathe as the crowd hurried to their cars to pull off before the police came and rounded them up. There were more than twenty police cars with their sirens on and flashlights beaming on the crowd.

As bad as the situation was, the thrill is what we all liked. It was illegal to be parked out in the streets with music blasting and drinking alcohol. But no one cared. The cops came to break it up every Sunday, but we still came out in the hundreds. All you could hear was car horns blowing as folks tried to squeeze their way out and get free.

"Lyric, take the back alley out," Kyra yelled out.

It took a matter of five minutes to drive behind the corner store to an open alley to get free. I looked behind us and saw cars had seen our getaway route and followed suit. We made it onto Lancaster where the streets were clear.

It seemed everyone let out a collective sigh of relief as Lyric made her detour and headed straight for Arlington Lake. The night had just begun.

£££

It was well after eleven when we pulled up to Arlington Lake. Many of the people who were on Miller had made their way here as well, and the party continued. Everyone jumped out of the car and proceeded to go their separate ways.

The lake was a place to hang out as if it were an outside club. Whether you were as old as fifty or as young as thirteen, everyone made their way here on Sunday nights. I spotted Mr. Joe who owned one of the oldest barbecue restaurants on the south side cooking up some hot links.

"Mr. Joe, come on and hook me up with one. How much is it?" I asked, already drooling at the mouth.

"Hey, Cookie, what are you doing out here? Does Della know you out here?" He laughed and started to cough as the smoke ambushed his face when he opened the grill. Sierra laughed at his question. I hated the fact that almost everyone as old as hell knew my mama.

I didn't realize how well-known Mama was until I started hanging out in places Mama used to back in the day. Fort Worth used to be so small that everyone knew one another somehow and in some way. And even now that it's almost tripled in population, the same folks we knew coming up still monitored the city and those in it like it was back in the day.

"Mr. Joe, Mama knows I'm here with my sis and my friends. Can I just get a hot link?" I tried to hide my attitude. Although he wasn't my boss, we all grew up knowing to respect your elders and to hold your tongue.

I selected my white bread and held it out for him to drop me a link in it. Then I passed him $2.50. Walking away, I heard my name called, and Sierra and I looked around for who it was.

"Hey, isn't that mystery guy from Miller?" Sierra asked.

I was drooling over my hot link, but seeing him again made my whole mouth salivate. "Usher, ooppps, I mean Denzel, what are you doing here?" We all laughed out at my obvious joke.

"I got your Usher, girl. Just my luck to see you in two places in one night. What you got there? Something from Mr. Joe?"

Taking a bite I mouthed, "And you know it. Best food in town."

"Well, me and my crew posted up over there."

I shrugged my shoulders, knowing I wasn't going to follow him nowhere. I started to sense Sierra's uncertainty, and I knew why. Ever since she was raped, I made sure to not be alone with guys I didn't know.

"Look, Denzel, you can walk with us if you want. Our crew is over there," I said pointing toward the lake. I noticed Lyric and Lynn in

67

the crowd about to get on a boat. Sierra and I, along with Denzel, rushed over to get on too.

The boat held about twenty other people. The bartender started to pass drinks around. I took a champagne cup, and Sierra and I raced to the top of the boat to get a full view of the lake.

"Girl, if our classmates could see us up here living it up," Sierra screamed.

I felt a hand wrap around my waist and looked back to notice it was Denzel. "You ladies look beautiful in the moonlight."

"Well, this I know," I boasted. We all clicked glasses and took a sip of our drinks. It wasn't long until Sierra started talking it up with a guy as I got entangled in my conversation with Denzel. We stayed on that boat for another hour listening and dancing to music and not having a care in the world.

When it was well after two a.m., we all hopped in the van to start the trail of dropping everyone off at their houses. Lyric called out to me and said, "Cookie, Carlos has been blowing up my phone."

"Let me see," I said grabbing the phone out of her hand. I read six missed calls. The last one was placed thirty minutes ago. I flipped open the phone and called him back.

"Carlos, what's up?" I was agitated about his numerous phone calls. I felt as if he was trying to take the fun out of my night just because we were dating.

"It's almost three in the morning. *Now* you call me back?" His voice was low as if he had been asleep.

"Carlos, you kept calling all night. I was busy. You just called thirty minutes ago. Why? What's up?"

"I didn't want you out tonight."

"Why? Don't start changing up on me now. I'm the same Cookie as I have ever been and will stay this way."

"What do you need to go out for anyway? I could of came and got you."

"Why are you acting all different now anyways? I can see me at home waiting for you to call or come and never show up as always. You just don't want me to have any fun."

"You know what, Cookie? I would have come because ..." His voice trailed off, and he cut off his sentence.

"Because of what?"

"Nothing. Just forget it."

"No, you been calling this phone all night. Say what's on your mind."

"I figured you would have been having sex with someone tonight!" he screamed.

Shocked, I said, "Huh?"

"You weren't a virgin, Cookie, the other night when we had sex. I could tell you had sex before, and you weren't tight."

"Oh my God, are you accusing me of something?" I tried to act innocent but was more shocked with the fact that he knew I had sex with someone else.

"Cookie, who are you sleeping with? I thought we promised to wait on each other. Remember, I asked you to only allow me to touch you in that way."

"Yeah, I remember, but I also remember you standing me up, not calling, missing in action, and all that. What do you expect me to do?"

"So because I wasn't there for a little while you go and have sex with someone else?"

"It's not like I just picked someone off the street, Carlos."

"Wait. Is you telling me you are in a relationship with someone?"

I started to get really agitated. I was almost sixteen, and I was being asked to be in a committed relationship. I wanted to have fun, not be an old maid.

"Carlos, can we talk about this tomorrow? Come and see me after school."

"I'll think about it." And then the line went dead. I flipped the phone shut and lay back in my seat.

"Carlos tripping?" Sierra asked. I forgot anyone else was in the car for a minute. I nodded my head yes and closed my eyes, letting the sleep take over the rest of the ride.

Tamika Newhouse

Things Change Like Day and Night

While sorting through things to wear in my closet I heard a knock on the door. I called out to see if Mama wanted me to get it. She stated she was in the bathroom, so I rushed out of my room into the living room and looked through the peephole to see who was at our door.

I had to blink again. No way was this man at my door. I asked, "Who is it?" knowing good and well I knew who it was.

I was annoyed. I didn't want to sit down and talk to him and act like I was happy to see him, so I took a deep breath and placed my hand on the knob. I gave the fakest smile I could create and said, "Hey, Daddy, long time no see."

"Hey, Latoya, how you been?" For as long as I can remember, Howard, my daddy, has always called me Latoya. I guess if he called me Cookie that would mean he knew me, which he doesn't.

"I'm good." I slid out of the doorway to let him by. I pointed for him to sit on the couch. "Give me a minute, Daddy, and I'll be right back."

I hated calling him Daddy, but that was the best title I could come up with without being disrespectful. I marched back to Lyric's room and knocked on her door.

"What?" she called out.

"I just wanted you to know that your father is here."

"*My* father? Who? Howard is out there right now?"

"Yes, so get off the phone. I ain't talking to him alone."

I closed her door and marched over to Mama's room, where she had made herself comfortable and naked again. "Mama, put on some clothes, please. Our daddy is here."

"What is he doing here? Why didn't he call?" She rose up, trying to find her closest gown. I shrugged my shoulders and told her she didn't have to come out front if she didn't want to and that I would handle it.

Making my trail back to the torture chamber that held my sperm donor, I took another deep breath and planted my fake smile on again. The sooner I talked to him the sooner he would leave. Don't get me wrong. I cared about what happened to him, like if he lived or died, but I didn't need to see or talk to him, for that matter. I mean, what would we talk about?

I noticed Lyric had already walked in. She seemed excited to see him. I could only imagine. I had no good memories of him unlike Lyric. I was just a baby when he left Mama. I have a brother who is exactly the same age as me, which explains what kind of man he was.

"Latoya, you are looking all grown up now," he said, reaching in for a hug.

I sat down on the couch across from him and said, "Yep, school is out, you know, and my birthday is only a couple weeks away. I'll be sixteen."

"Oh yea, that's right. Let me see what I got here for you." He reached into his pocket and pulled out a twenty-dollar bill. I wanted to throw that bill in his face, but figured he ain't given me anything in years; I guess I'll take it.

"Well, gee, thanks, Daddy; I'll make sure to give this to Mama for some gas in her van," I said sarcastically.

Lyric interrupted and said, "So, what's up? What are you doing here?"

"Well, Cleo and I are going to be having a fish fry at the house today. I wanted to see if you two wanted to come through. Your brothers and sister will be there too."

I know he ain't trying to put us together like the Brady Bunch.

I was agitated inside. I did not want to go anywhere with him, but I knew Mama would make me go. Go and see you brothers and sister, she would say. But I don't know them, I would say. But at the end, I would still be forced to go.

"I think we can manage that. What time does it start?" Lyric asked. I wanted to slap her across the face.

"It'll start around five, so I'll see you girls there?"

"Daddy, couldn't you have called and asked this?" I said. I clearly had an attitude. I held a strong dislike for him because he was never there for us and I couldn't hide that fact.

"Well, yeah, but I was in the neighborhood and hadn't stopped by in a while."

"Daddy, you live ten miles away. That's always in the neighborhood," I shot back.

"Cookie!" Lyric called out, trying to get me to shut up.

"My bad. I'm just saying, it's been a couple years since I've seen you, and you talking about you in the neighborhood and all. I don't get it." I shrugged my shoulders, disregarding the fact that I was disrespecting the man who donated his sperm to give me life.

I could hear Mama walking down the hallway, "Hey, Howard. Thought I would come and save you from Cookie and her mouth."

74

They gave each other a casual hug, and then Mama took a seat next to me.

"No problem, Della, I understand. But girls, I want you to know I want us to get to know each other."

Yeah, now that you only got two years to pay child support on me, and Lyric is damn near twenty-one.

"That's fine, Daddy. Cookie and I will be by to see you and our brothers," Lyric added giving him a hug as he walked out the door.

I stayed planted in my seat because unlike Lyric, I wasn't excited to see him or his secondary family. *How you marry your mistress and expect us to be one big happy family?*

When the coast was clear, Mama turned to me and gave me the evil eye. "What?" I bashfully said.

"Dang, you are so mean, Cookie," Lyric yelled out.

"Don't go there. Y'all know I don't like that man. What do I have to pretend for?"

"Because he is your father," Mama added.

"Correction, he is my daddy. A father is someone you call and celebrate on Father's Day; a father is someone I know. And that man I do not know."

"Just get dressed and be ready." Lyric marched out of the living room.

"Come on, Mama, don't make me go. I don't want to be around them folks."

"Cookie, I want you to go, have fun, and watch your mouth. You only got one father, and you got other brothers and sisters you need to know."

75

"Mama, he don't even know how many kids he got," I shot back. She looked at me as if she wanted to slap the taste out of my mouth, and I quickly shut up. Before I knew it, I was in the passenger seat of Mama's van riding with Lyric to our daddy's house, and I wasn't happy about it.

£££

The scene at Daddy's house to me would scream a "hot mess," but in actuality, it was just his family. When walking in, Lyric immediately started to make her rounds around the room saying hello to aunts and uncles I didn't know and speaking to our brothers.

I proceeded to be nice and make my way to my grandparents because in true form, I was happy to see them. I hadn't seen them since we visited them in Lubbock several years ago.

"Is this little Latoya?" I heard my aunt Jen scream. She was already drunk.

Not wanting to hug her because she had the skin of a crocodile and a beard out of this world, I sucked it in, held my breath, and leaned into her embrace. "Hey, Aunt Jen," I mumbled and planted on my award-winning smile.

"Girl, you look just like your Aunt Wilma." I always heard that from the time I reached puberty. My Aunt Wilma, who I could never remember, obviously resembled exactly how I looked, and when I got around Howard's family, they made sure to tell me every time I saw them.

My younger brother walked over to me and gave me a friendly hand shake and told me where the food was, and I wasted no time getting a plate. I may have not liked my daddy, but his cooking was another thing. He was one of the best!

76

After grabbing a couple plates for myself, being a true foody and acting greedy as hell, I found a spot to sit and stuff my face and started taking in the scene. Cousins and aunts and uncles I hadn't seen in a while flooded his living room.

My daddy's wife, who wasn't a bad person at all, came over and dropped a piece of apple pie in my lap. In that moment I wanted to give her a big wet kiss on her cheek. If I hated you, you could absolutely win me over with some food.

After I had eaten, a few hours rolled by and I was contemplating walking those ten miles back home. Days like this I wish I had a car. "You enjoying yourself, Latoya?"

I looked up and saw my daddy taking a seat next to me. We were seated in his swing that was planted in the middle of his front yard. The summer heat was weaning down, and I felt it was a perfect time to get away from all the noise his family was making, but surprisingly, he met me out here.

"I enjoyed myself, and the food was good, and your wife did an excellent job with that pie. You think I can get a slice to take home?"

"Sure. I'm so happy to see you and your sister come out."

I smiled at him and managed to look my daddy in the eyes. He was getting old. Still handsome but old.

"You know I still got my issues with you, but it was good to see you and the family."

He nodded his head that he understood. "I know, but this is the way to work through them." I still kept thinking that he was too late. I was damn near an adult, and Lyric was already grown. I wasn't a child anymore. I didn't want a relationship now.

77

"I guess."

"You know you can call me anytime."

I nodded my head that I knew that but what would we talk about really? I proceeded to start the conversation off with how my sophomore year in school went and how I was coping with Trent's death. He had missed so much I didn't realize I had been talking for an hour when Lyric came and told me it was time to go. I hugged my daddy good-bye and told him I loved him, which I did. But I knew deep down I wasn't going to see or hear from him for a long time, as usual.

Tamika Newhouse

I Got To Be The One You Love

I held the remote in my hand and turned the speaker up to its highest volume and started singing to Jagged Edge's song "Gotta Be." "You make me whole, you make me right. Don't ever wanna think about you leaving my life."

"Cookie, shut up!" I heard Lyric scream from her room. I laughed out knowing that most folks couldn't stand my voice, but I loved to sing. Wasn't my fault God didn't give me a voice of a humming bird.

In the midst of my singing I heard the house phone ring. Rushing over to it, I picked it up out of breath.

"Dang, Cook, what are you doing over there?" I smiled from ear to ear hearing Carlos's voice.

"Hey, Carlos, what's up? I'm just over here singing."

He started to laugh out and said, "Please, don't let me hear any of what's coming out of your mouth."

"Whatever, boy. I can sing just like Brandy."

"Brandy the dog, for sure." He was laughing so hard I started to get mad and slammed the phone down in its cradle. I knew he would call back and when he did, I let it ring four times before I picked it up.

"Hello," I said, acting as if I didn't know who it was.

"I'm sorry, baby; damn. I was just playing. Your voice is beautiful." I could tell he was still laughing but overlooked it because I knew my voice was horrible anyhow.

"So what's up?"

80

"I'm coming to get you to take you to get something for your birthday." I wanted to ask him if he was still mad at me for not being a virgin but since the conversation was a couple weeks ago I decided not to.

"Sure. I'll tell Mama I'm going out with you, and I'll be ready in a bit. When are you coming?"

"I'm on my way now, so please don't take all day."

"Fine. Mama may wanna see you and say hey anyway. I see you in a minute."

"I love you," he said.

I smiled and said, "I love you too."

Clicking the phone back in its cradle I heard Mama say, "Who are you saying I love you to?"

"Oh, that was Carlos, Mama. He wants to take me to the mall for my birthday. Is that OK? Plus, you know I didn't get him anything for his graduation."

"Hmm, I see. When is he coming over?"

"In about an hour, so please don't be naked." I laughed and ran back to my room to find an outfit to put on.

"Where are you going off to?" Lyric said standing in my doorway.

"Carlos is coming to get me and take me to the mall. Why?"

"Mama said you can go?" She turned her head and yelled down the hallway, "Mama, I thought you said Cookie couldn't date till she was sixteen, and obviously, she got a head start."

Rolling my eyes, I said, "Don't hate on me." I walked up to her and closed my door, using every last second I had getting ready for my day with Carlos.

81

My hair was freshly permed, and I wore it with big loose curls all over and complemented it with a headband. My new sundress that had an opening on my back was matched with my new, white, four-inch heels. I had a new body spray Mama had gotten me from Bath and Body Works called Heaven. And I smelled just like heaven too.

Oddly, I was still shy around Carlos sometimes and today was no different. I was paranoid about the way I smiled, if my breath stank, if my hair was on point, were my heels to tall, and yada yada.

He looked at me and said, "Just relax, Cookie; you look fine. I can tell you over there examining your look. I don't care if you were in a rag. You'll still be my baby." He took my hand and kissed the back of it.

I smiled and leaned back in the car seat feeling more comfortable. I noticed him taking a detour. "Are we going in here to eat?" I said looking toward Olive Garden.

"Yep, I told you I'm going to treat you for your sweet sixteen, didn't I?" He leaned toward me for a kiss. I obliged kissing him softly. We both climbed out of the car making our way to the main entrance hand in hand. I had to give it to him; he was making me feel like a queen today.

Taking our seats at the dining table, I pulled out my menu knowing I was going to get my same old lasagna.

"Order what you want, babe; it's on me. No budget."

"Boy, don't tell me nothing like that. I *will* order it up just because," I teased.

82

The waiter came over and asked us our drinks. I also ordered an appetizer since I'm never able to get one when Mama and I go out to eat.

"So your birthday is tomorrow. What do you have planned?"

"Nothing really. I think I'm going to hang with Lyric and the crew." I sensed his unhappiness with my answer.

"I'm trying to not crowd you and all, but I hate it when you are out with Lyric. I know she ain't on the straight and narrow, and plus, I have seen Lynn with more money lately. I don't think her and Lyric are legit, if you know what I mean."

I took a sip of my tea to not comment on the matter, which to him was a dead giveaway.

"Cookie, are you involved in whatever they're doing?"

"What do you mean?" *Shoot, wrong reply.*

"Cookie, I heard around that they into some check shit. Tell me you aren't doing that too. I mean, I noticed your new clothes and shit, but I didn't think you would be getting down like that."

"Can we change the subject?"

Carlos leaned forward, placing his head in hands as if he had a headache. "You cheating and have sex with who knows, staying out all night, and now writing these checks. I'm trying to be patient and understanding, but how can I leave, knowing you doing all of this?"

I bypassed the sex allegation and said, "Leaving to go where?"

"I am going to Atlanta for school. I wanted tell you that today."

"When?"

"In August. Cookie, what's going on with you?"

"Nothing is going on that I can't handle. I can't believe you're leaving."

"If Mama would let me take you with me, I would. You know I love you, right?"

Clearly upset I said, "Yes, I know."

"Can I ask you who you had sex with? Cookie, I'm serious when I say I don't want you to be with anyone else."

"Carlos, I really don't want to talk about that. I am not comfortable with you asking me about it either."

"Well, shit, what am I supposed to do? Share you?"

"What do you mean, share? I get where you're coming from, and I'll try to be good, I promise."

He leaned in and grabbed my hand and said, "I love you. When you graduate, it's just going to be me and you, OK?"

Our food arrived, and it seemed we ate in silence with a million thoughts running through our heads. I was going into my junior year in high school, and although I loved Carlos, I knew deep down when he left for school I would be doing whatever I wanted.

I let the topic pass away and enjoyed the rest of our evening together. He topped it off by purchasing me four new outfits and a heart-shaped necklace. He said it was a promise that I had his heart. I told him without a doubt he had mine.

Tamika Newhouse

A Sour-Sixteen Indeed

I bent over not able to see much since the room was dark except for a lit night-light. I was anticipating his penetration from behind. It seemed every time we were together our bodies couldn't wait to connect. My insides boiled over as I felt his first touch.

"Baron, come on, please," I begged.

He moaned out as I felt him connect inside of me and our rhythms steadied out for more then thirty minutes when our bodies suddenly collapsed. I laughed out in satisfaction, taking a towel and wiping in between my legs.

"Hmm, Cookie, I love it when you come around. Happy Birthday, baby." Baron leaned forward on his bed placing a kiss on my lips.

"Well, thank you, love. I surely appreciate the gift you just gave me," I laughed.

I suddenly heard the echo of a Sunshine Anderson song from outside, and proceeded to place my underwear and jeans back on. "That's Lyric and the crew back, so come on."

Baron followed suit, placing his clothes back on. We walked outside hand in hand, and I heard Lyric yell, "Ew, stop acting like y'all in love and shit."

"So we about to go make a run. Y'all hop y'all ass in, then we'll go to the Roadhouse for Cookie's birthday," Johnny said.

Sliding in the back of Johnny's car I asked, "What run?"

"Johnny has to make this sale. He gonna pay for the dinner tonight," Lyric replied.

"Aw, thanks, Johnny." Baron closed the door, and we were off to complete Johnny's drug transaction.

£££

Driving into the Southside we turned on Baker Street. I instantly started to look around because everyone knew this was the drug zone for this part of town. But I didn't want to protest Johnny bringing us here, especially since he was paying for dinner.

We passed a few abandoned houses and stopped in front of the fourth house on the right. It was an old-looking house, and I honestly would have thought it was empty until just now. Johnny got out of the car and told us to wait a minute.

"This place looks infested from the outside," I complained. The quietness overtook us as five minutes turned into fifteen. I was starting to worry.

"Johnny is usually in and out by now," Baron complained. I heard his stomach growl and knew he was just as hungry as the rest of us.

"I don't know what's taking him so long. I'll text his phone and see," Lyric said.

"No, don't do that, Lyric. You know he can't use his phone when he dealing with these folks," Baron argued.

"What's that?" I yelled out in shock. We all jumped at the same time and looked toward the abandoned-looking house Johnny went into. "I swear I just saw someone pass us."

Lyric leaned over and immediately locked the doors. "See now, Cookie, you scaring the shit out of me."

"I got you, baby. You just scary, that's all." Baron reached over and placed his arm around my waist. I shook my head no. I knew I

87

wasn't crazy and seeing things. But my heart was hoping that maybe I was just seeing things.

Suddenly, we heard a tap on the back window. We all jumped and turned around. When I saw them I knew then that we were in a lot of trouble.

There were two guys who were sporting hoodies with masks over their faces. You couldn't make out if they were male or female, black or white. I just knew that whatever they wanted, it wasn't good.

"Don't open the door," Baron warned us. We looked each other in the eye. I searched for reassurance, but I saw that he was scared just like me.

One of them walked around to the driver's door and checked the lock. When they saw the door was locked, the person bent down and screamed at the window. "Open the damn door."

"Oh my God, what do they want?" Lyric cried out. She turned around and looked at me. Tears of fear immediately started to escape my eyes.

"OK, we got to get out of here before they start something," Baron said.

I looked around the car and noticed they were circling the car, and when I saw one reach for a stick, I knew he was going to try to break the window.

"Lyric, call 911."

"I don't know where we are," she replied hysterically.

"It doesn't matter! Tell them we are on Baker Street, and you see a woman getting attacked by two men. Do it now before they make their way in here," Baron yelled.

Pulling out her phone, Lyric hurried and dialed. I heard one of them say, "She's on the phone" and took the stick and slammed it against the back window.

I screamed, "Stop!"

Baron placed his arms around my body and squeezed me tightly. "Cookie, no matter what, if they get in here and I can't hold them down, I want you to keep kicking and screaming. Don't stop, you hear me? Fight back. I want you and Lyric to stay together and fight back, OK?"

Crying, I shook my head no as I heard the intruder hit the back window again, and this time the window cracked. I jumped and looked at the window with fear in my eyes.

"Cookie, do you hear me?" Baron said.

I looked over at Lyric who was telling the operator where we were, hoping the police didn't ignore us because of where we were. *I don't belong here.*

Baron looked around the car to see where they were, then said, "On the next hit, Cookie and Lyric, they are going to bust that window, then there's nothing separating us from them. I don't know what they want, but if I can find out and give it to them I will."

"OK, I'm staying on the phone, ma'am, but please hurry. They just spotted me and are coming," Lyric lied and said to the operator.

I gave Baron a tight squeeze, not wanting to let him go. He motioned for me to climb into the driver's seat. I did. I looked back outside and saw the intruder raise his hand. This time he held a gun.

I screamed out. Lyric and I gripped each other's hands. Baron yelled, "Get down."

Bam!

The back window shattered. Then one of the men said, "Get out now."

I could feel the blood rush through my veins as my heart started to beat uncontrollably. All I could see was the barrel of the gun pointed at us. Baron looked back toward me and mouthed the words, "I love you."

When I heard Baron unlock his back door I took a deep breath and held it. He stood outside the car face-to-face with the gunmen. Then one walked around to the other side of the door and leaned down on my side.

He tapped and pointed his index finger toward the lock, motioning for me to open the door. On the other side I heard Lyric whisper, "I have to hide my phone, ma'am. He's here. Please, hurry up." She put the phone in her bra.

I was crying so hard my vision was blurred. I took a glance toward Baron who was facing the end of a gun, and then toward Lyric who was crying and scared just as much as me. Eye to eye, I told her with my eyes that I was scared and that I loved her. I wanted her to know that in case this time around I wasn't as lucky. I placed my hand on the lock and lifted it up.

Lyric did the same to her side of the car and opened her door. I climbed out making sure I stood far away from the intruder. "Now, isn't that better? Next time you all should have just obeyed." He walked up to me, raised his hand, and slammed it down across my face, knocking me to the ground. I fell down on my back, my hand covering the spot he hit me.

I could hear Baron and Lyric call out to me. But with only the moonlight shining and no streetlights, I couldn't see them.

"What is it that you want?" Baron asked.

"Your boy Johnny is low on cash. Seems he needs to compensate us or we have a serious problem."

"How much?" Lyric asked.

"About $300. Now, we were going to take the car, but since we had to bust the window out we have to knock off $75. Do you have $75 for me?" he asked.

I heard Baron and Lyric say no.

I rolled over toward the car and saw where Baron and Lyric were standing. I heard footsteps behind me and saw the intruder bend down, "Looks like we gonna have to use another resource. Yo', dog, what you think about this little bitch here? She looks like she's worth $75." He laughed.

Baron yelled out, "No, not her. Look, I can get you the $75; I can get you more than that. Just leave her alone. Please." My heart started to rattle as I began to understand what he wanted.

"Sir, if you let us get you the money ..." Lyric begged.

"You looking kind of hot too, with them big-ass titties. What you think, dog?"

"I don't know. Which one you want?"

"Where's Johnny? He'll tell you we can get you more money," Baron added.

"Johnny can't talk right now." I heard Lyric start to cry out.

I jumped when I felt the intruder's hand brush my leg. I kicked his hand away. "Now don't make me get rough with you," he threatened. I slid my body under the car door and screamed out no.

I glanced over and saw Lyric drop to the floor to see where I was. "Cookie, come here."

91

"Bitch, get up," I heard him say.

I couldn't see, but I could tell that Baron was fighting with the other guy. *"Cookie, no matter what, if they get in here and I can't hold them down, I want you to keep kicking and screaming. Don't stop, you hear me. Fight back."*

I took my right heel and kicked it where I saw his head. He fell back in agony, reaching out for my leg. When he caught me, I yelled out to Lyric to pull me. I could feel the gravel pierce and tear the skin off of my back as Lyric grabbed my hands, and with all her strength she pulled me out from under the car.

I glanced over seeing Baron and the guy tangled in a huge scuffle. "Run!" he managed to shout.

I didn't want to leave him, but Lyric pulled my arm and like the wind, we were running for our lives. We ran and didn't look back. Racing along, Lyric pulled out her phone from her bra and yelled, "Hello, yes, I'm still here. Where the fuck are the police?"

I glanced back and noticed we were several houses away from where we started, and then I heard a blast.

Pow!

Pow!

Pow!

"No!" I screamed out. I screamed so hard my throat started to ache as I cried hysterically.

"Oh my God, miss, we're on Shaw now. I don't know exactly where we are, but it's in between some houses. Look, here, just send an ambulance. We had to leave a friend, and we just heard gunshots."

All kinds of thoughts started to run through my head, thinking about Baron and if I was going to lose him like I lost Trent. My hand

92

wiped away massive amounts of tears, then I noticed a patrol car pass us. I didn't wait for Lyric to notice too. I just took off running toward it.

Before it got away, I slammed my hand on the back of the car. The officer stopped and hopped out. "Are you the two women I got the call about?"

Running up behind me Lyric said, "Yes. Our friends are down here, sir." We hopped in the back of his patrol car and turned down Baker Street from where we just ran.

"It's that last house down there, sir. See, our car is parked ..." Lyric's words trailed off when she didn't see the car. I leaned forward, trying to look through the bars in the police car and noticed Baron on the ground.

"Sir, that's my boyfriend right there."

The police officer spoke into his radio and requested an ambulance because, just like me, he could see that Baron was shot.

He swerved and parked his car, and I yelled for him to open my door. He didn't.

In a matter of seconds, an ambulance pulled up with its sirens blaring and another patrol car arrived at the same time. My eyes were set on Baron as I saw a paramedic lean over him and turn his body over. *Is he alive? Is he alive?* I chanted that question over and over in my head. I watched their every move.

Lyric and I were planted at the tip of our seats wondering if Baron was alive. We watched them load him on a gurney and place him in the ambulance. I saw an officer run out of the house and yell, "We got another one."

"Oh my God—Johnny," Lyric cried out. The ambulance with Baron pulled off and another pulled up. The paramedics rushed in with their gear in tow and in a matter of minutes, we could see Johnny. Dead.

I closed my eyes and said a prayer. My insides started to boil over, and I bent down and threw up all the contents of my stomach. I was not able to hold anything in.

£££

John Peter Smith Hospital is where I was born. It was also the central location we went for Mama's checkups. But today, it became the place I hated. Walking in, the officer told us that our friends were in surgery but both were alive—barely.

I breathed a sigh of relief. And one by one, a cop came up to us to ask us what happened. We could only tell what we knew, but who and why is where we went dry. When we were left alone, I took my head into my hands and cried out. Lyric came up to me and placed her arm around my shoulders and cried with me.

After ten minutes of sobbing, the anger set in. "Never again," I said looking at Lyric.

"What?" she asked.

"Tonight we could have been raped, all because I'm riding with you and your drug-dealing boyfriend. And for what?"

Lyric looked at me with nothing to say. I didn't blame her, just the company she kept. "Why must you pick these types of guys? Never again, I tell you."

"If it wasn't for Johnny, you wouldn't have met Baron." She was right, but after tonight, I started to wonder if meeting him was worth it. *He could die tonight.*

94

I brought my hand to my eye that was aching and felt a lump from where I was hit. The scratches on my back were starting to ache too; I told one of the cops that I needed a nurse.

"You might as well call Mama now," I said, getting up from my seat and following the receptionist to a nurse's station.

£££

After we were hugged and asked if we were OK, Mama's fist started to connect to Lyric's stomach and face. I asked her to calm down, but that didn't stop me from being the recipient of a few of her blows. I could tell she limited the amount of hits she gave me because I was clearly wounded.

"I can't believe this shit, and you, Lyric, supposed to be watching Cookie. I ought to knock the shit out of you." Now if you didn't really know Mama you would be wondering why a churchgoing woman like her would be striking and cussing her kids out. But as I said before, Mama was a churchgoing woman but could knock you into the next century.

After being asked to calm down by the police, I could tell Mama's blood pressure was up because she stumbled to find a seat. I cried, knowing that this situation wasn't helping my mother's health. She was already sick.

On the hospital bed I cramped over, holding my stomach in pain from the pounds Mama laid on me. The room was quiet as Mama and Lyric were outside my room, but it wasn't quiet enough for me to hear the nurses talking to them about Johnny and Baron.

I couldn't hear a thing so I hopped off the bed, limping, and cracked open the door. "If you want to see Mr. Baron Taylor, he's in

95

ICU Room 3 and Mr. Johnny Richardson is in ICU Room 7," I heard the nurse say.

I ran and hopped back on the bed before anyone saw me. That same nurse walked in and gave me a courteous smile. "And Ms. James, how are we doing?"

I nodded my head OK.

"Well, the doctors want to hold you over for just one night. I told your mother and sister already. They'll be in shortly." I nodded that I understood.

Out walked the nurse, and in walked Mama. She leaned down and gave me a hug. "I'm sorry, Mama," I whispered.

"I'll be back with some clothes for you tomorrow. We'll talk about this later." She walked out and didn't say another word. I reached over and cut the light out, needing to rest and forget about what could have happened to me tonight.

Just as I was about to go to sleep, Lyric walked in. "Hey, sis."

"Hey."

"I'm about to go see Johnny and Baron, and then go home with Mama."

"Can you do me a favor?"

"Yea, what?"

"Call Carlos for me and tell him to come and see me please."

"Are you sure? I mean, you were with ..." Her words trailed off.

"Yes, I just want him here. Tell him that." She hugged me good-bye and walked out. I again turned over and started my quest for some rest.

£££

I woke up to the sound of footsteps and people chattering. It was dark, and I could tell I wasn't in my own bed. I looked up saw a machine beeping. *Where am I?*

I turned over and looked around the room, and then last night started to flash through my mind. *I'm in the hospital.* I looked up and noticed the clock on the wall. Four thirty.

I looked out the window and noticed that it was still dark, so it had to have been four thirty in the morning. I brought my hand to my head that was starting to pound and felt the bandage over my eye. *That's right. I was hit. Wait, where's Baron?*

I started to retrace my memory, and then the nurse's statement came back to mind. He's in ICU. I pulled back my bedsheets and searched for my clothes. I found them in a white plastic bag marked JPS Hospital and proceeded to slip on my jeans and shirt.

Once I had on my sneakers, I cracked opened my door and poked my head out for a nurse. The coast was clear. I walked out of my hospital room without catching anyone's suspicion.

Walking out into the lobby I look for the directory that told me what floor ICU was on. *The fourth floor. OK, where are the elevators?* Locating the elevators, I hopped on and pressed number 4.

When the doors swung open the floor was completely quiet. I knew it wasn't visiting hours so I had to sneak my way to Baron's room. I was glad to see I was immediately by room number 1. I took a deep breath and ran toward room number 3 to bypass the nurses' station. I swung around the room curtain and instantly heard the beeping of the machine.

I brought my hand to my mouth and tried to muffle out my cries. Baron wasn't awake. He was breathing with a machine, and I knew this situation from the past. I had suffered the death of my god-brother, favorite cousin, and two uncles within a two-year span. I knew death when I saw it coming.

I started talking to God immediately. I knew I was wrong for praying to him now when I needed him, but what else was I supposed to do? I had some love for Baron. Hell, I didn't want to see him die.

I walked up alongside his bed and placed my hand on his shoulder. *He helped save me. He fought for Lyric and me to get away.* I wiped away my tears and leaned down to kiss him on his forehead. His face wasn't recognizable. It was swollen with cuts and bruises.

I placed my hands in his and whispered, "Thank you for being there for me. And now I'm going to be here for you."

I wanted so badly to know if he felt my presence. I started to wonder if his mother and brother knew. I knew Lyric would have called them by now.

The quietness and the sound of the ventilator rising up and down started to work my nerves. I was a nervous wreck. I placed my head down in my lap and drifted off to sleep. It felt comforting to be next to Baron, to know that he was still here in some way.

Tamika Newhouse

I Never Saw This Coming

It had been two weeks since Baron and Johnny were shot. Luckily, Johnny was out of the woods, but that wasn't the same for Johnny and Lyric's relationship. It turned downhill for some reason, but I didn't bother to ask since I was still upset about being so close to rape and death.

Baron, however, was in the same condition. A few times I snuck on the city bus to go and see him, skipping a few classes here and there. I became emotionally distant, which is why I hadn't spent much time with Carlos, who was upset with me anyhow.

You see, I wasn't supposed to be with Baron, according to Carlos. I was supposed to be with him only. Of course, that's when he decided to come around because, unlike him, I didn't have a car and could come and go when I chose.

It was knocking on the month of July with only a couple more months left in the summer, so I decided to take Mama up on her trip to go visit Jayla and Lola in Corpus Christi, Texas.

Hugging Sierra good-bye and not even bothering to call Carlos, I hopped in Mama's van, and she, Lyric, and I hit Highway 35 on our way to a city I've come to know as The Hellhole. It was a pretty city and all, with a beachfront, but lacked anything black, and there was nothing really to do there.

I lay my head down on the backseat and drifted off into sleep, dreaming of a time when I felt life was easier and I didn't have these grown-up problems. At least, that's what I thought—until I arrived in Corpus Christi.

£££

Well, after six hours I looked up and noticed Mama pulling up in front of Lola's house. We hadn't visited in a long time. I noticed Lola open her front door and immediately I was confused, thinking it was a white woman. She was lighter than light, brighter than bright. For years, folks thought she was a white woman with red hair. I guess it's something you never get used to.

I hopped out of the car, walked up to her, and said, "I got to pee."

"Well, hello, to you too, Cookie." I leaned in and gave her a hug, happy to see her, but the squeeze didn't help my bladder. I rushed in and found my way to the toilet.

Washing my hands after I was done, I heard the usual hi's and how you been's. It's been approximately a year since our last trip. I walked out of the bathroom searching for Jayla, who always seemed like she was OK if she saw us or not. Never mind the fact we grew up together from the time we were born.

I noticed her on the phone and I walked in and said, "Hey, Jayla, what's up?"

"Hey, Cookie, give me one minute," she said, holding up her finger, signaling she was on an important call.

Important call, my ass. She was only a year younger than Lyric and two years older than me and acted as if she were 30. I shrugged my shoulders and made a beeline to the kitchen, because I knew Lola had cooked something.

Noticing a plate full of fried chicken, I grabbed a paper plate, slapped three drumsticks on it, and dove into the potato salad.

"That's all you ever do is come over here and eat," Lola said, taking the plate out of my hand and finishing up preparing my meal.

"Now, Lola, you know I love to eat." I took the filled plate in my hand and dove into it even before I took my seat in front of the TV.

Not even five minutes rolled around and I saw Lola's husband walk in. I put on my Miss America smile, because truth is, I didn't really care for him, and said, "Hey, Mr. Hill, how are you?" I knew good and well he was about to talk to me for a good fifteen minutes. I just wanted him to hurry up with his old folk's stories so I could finish my food.

Before I knew it, he started off with his narration. "You know, Cookie, you are getting so big. Just look at that puffy face of yours, all grown up and looking like a young woman. I'm just so proud of you and Lyric. Didn't know it was going to take me this long to see y'all. But y'all here, and that's all that matters, right? Hey, there, what you eating? Did Lola cook us up a meal? Let me go get a plate and I'll be right back."

Will this Negro shut the hell up so I can eat?

"Oh no, that's OK, Mr. Hill, go ahead and get your plate and take your time," I yelled out. Quickly, I picked up my plate and made a dash for the back room. I couldn't suffer through one of his boring stories again.

Back in the guest room Jayla walked in. "Hey, Cookie, so tell me what's been going on?" She playfully tapped my leg and laughed. "Girl, look at you. What you been doing? Your hips have done spread."

"It's called growing up, Jayla."

"Yea, sure." She eyed my plate. "Mama done cooking. I'm gonna get a plate and come right back."

102

I heard Lyric's laugh before she entered. "Yea, your hips spread all right."

Rolling my eyes I said, "I got a bona fide dime piece here, my dear. Don't be jealous." I bit into my chicken and turned on the TV.

It didn't take me long to eat and curl up on the guest bed and fall asleep. I guess a long ride will do that to you.

£££

After spending four days in Corpus Christi, I was glad when we started to load up the van to head back to Funkytown. I had called Sierra already to tell her to be ready for me because I wanted to go out. It was fun seeing Lola and Jayla, but now it was time to head back home. I pulled my pillow and blanket next to me, curled up on my seat in the back of the van, and flipped a CD into my CD player, and allowed 112 to sing about Cupid.

It was well after eight p.m. when we pulled up in front of our house. Dragging myself out of the car, I rushed out, asking Mama for the house keys to get to the phone. After opening the front door, I pulled the cordless into my hand and dialed Sierra's number. "Heifer, I'm home."

"Hey, girl, I was wondering if y'all got back yet."

"I'm gonna have Lyric drop me off over there, OK?"

"Yea, OK, but bring a bag of popcorn. I know Mama got some over there." I laughed and said I would, hanging up the phone and yelling for Lyric to come on.

£££

"So I'm glad you're back in town. It gives us the perfect opportunity to meet up with Jared and his homeboy Charles," Sierra said, holding up a T-shirt to see which one she wanted to wear.

103

"You slut. I came to hang with you," I laughed. She threw a pillow and laughed along with me. "So this is your new boo in your life, huh?"

"For now; shoot, I'm only sixteen, and I honestly want to have fun. Just be smart about it, you know?"

In her bed I rolled over on my side and nodded my head in agreement. I suddenly felt a rush of heat. I had felt this way a couple days ago, but overlooked it. Sierra looked over toward me and said, "Girl, what's wrong with you? You look like you about to pass out."

Pulling my shirt off and falling back on the bed with just my bra on, I mumbled, "I just got hot all of a sudden. I feel like I'm going to pass out or throw up." Sierra walked into her bathroom and placed a towel in some cold water. After wringing it out, she came back and put it on my head.

"You don't feel hot."

I felt a sense of faintness and rolled over as the contents of my stomach started to spray all over the floor.

"Oh my God!" Sierra ran over and grabbed her trash can, placing it underneath my mouth.

"Damn, what's up? It must be that long-ass ride," I managed to say.

Covering her nose to block the stench, Sierra mumbled, "That, or you're pregnant." Her face showed that she was completely joking, but when she said it, my mind started to race back over the last few days. Not to mention my irregular period that came every now and then hadn't come at all this month.

"Pregnant?" I whispered.

"Wait, Cook, I was joking."

I started to remember Mr. Hill's comments about my puffy face, and Jayla saying my hips had spread. Then there was the urge to eat everything in sight. Now this. I was throwing up. *Could I REALLY be pregnant?*

Wiping my mouth with the cold towel, I sat up and looked at Sierra, who was watching my every move. "I think we should get a pregnancy test. I'm sitting here thinking about what you just said, and it scares me because it makes sense."

"Oh my God, Cookie, are you serious? Who have you been having sex with?"

"Just Baron and Carlos."

"*Both* of them?"

Rolling my eyes I said, "Yeah; don't judge me, OK? It's just been those two."

"Now you know I'm not judging you at all. Let me go grab some money out of my wallet, and I'll walk to Albertson's and get you a test kit."

Laying my head back onto her pillow I closed my eyes to hide my tears. What if I was pregnant, then what? What would I do then? Would the baby be Baron's or Carlos's? Then I thought of Mama and instantly got scared. She was going to whoop my ass. I couldn't go home and tell her I was pregnant.

It was almost an hour before Sierra made it back. "Are you ready?" I shook my head no but snatched the test out of her hand and went to the bathroom.

The box read to pee on the stick for ten seconds and let it sit for one minute and read the results. Sounded too simple if you ask me for something so serious.

I pulled the stick out and pulled down my pants, squatting over the toilet. After I was done, I sealed the stick back up with its top and placed it on the counter.

I wasn't halfway done pulling up my pants when Sierra opened the door. "Is it ready?"

"No. Can I pull my pants up? Dang."

She took a step back but didn't bother to close the door again. I ran the water over my hands to wash them and counted to 60 in my head. *Just breathe, girl. This is going to be a no-brainer. No way are you pregnant.*

"OK, Cookie, it's been about two minutes. Do you want me to read it?"

Too nervous to look, I nodded my head yes.

It seemed like an eternity passed by as I watched her pick up the stick and the box to read its directions. She didn't smile; she didn't start to praise at all. Then I knew.

"Sierra, is it a plus on the stick or not?" My insides were fluttering. My knees were weak, and my head was light. I was going to pass out from nervous anticipation.

"Damn, Cookie. It's positive."

Tamika Newhouse

God Never Make's A Mistake

I didn't feel like wearing my usual tight-fitted jeans and halter shirt. I now knew why they weren't quite fitting the way I wanted them to anyway. Yesterday after taking the test I didn't want to do anything but lie around, so Sierra had called Mama to let her know I was staying over.

It was now in the morning, and I was searching through Sierra's drawers for some baggy pants and a big T-shirt. I wasn't in the mood for dressing up. Standing in her mirror looking over my hand-me-down attire, my eyes stopped at my stomach. *Is there a baby in here?* I brought my hand to my stomach as tears started to fall from my eyes. I was interrupted when Sierra's door opened.

"Hey, are you OK?" she asked.

I plopped down on her bed and brought my hands up to cover my face. "I'll live for now. Did you call Carlos for me?"

"Yea, he still sounds like he's mad at you for being with Baron, but he heard the seriousness in my voice and is on his way. Do you want something to eat? My mama just made sausage, eggs, and biscuits."

"Just a biscuit and a sausage to put something in my stomach." As she walked out I turned around and opened her bedroom window to let the summer breeze come through. My mind was running a million miles a minute when I saw Carlos's Monte Carlo pull up.

Sierra poked her head in the door and said, "Here's your food, and Carlos just pulled up."

It felt like a walk to an execution chair. I took the food in my hand and nervously walked to the front door and stepped out on the porch. Just seeing him made me want to cry. He looked so cute and walked with swagger. I started to think that after he found out I was pregnant we wouldn't be us anymore.

I motioned for us to go sit in the hammock. He followed.

"So what are you doing over here?" he asked. I couldn't tell if he was still upset with me at all. His face was blank.

"I needed some time away from the routine, you know? Being here, I found out some things about myself."

"What do you mean?"

I was hesitating at first, but when I spoke I wanted to read his reaction to get the true meaning of how he was feeling so I turned to look him in his face. "I came over here to hang out with Sierra after getting back into town. But then I got sick."

"Sick how?"

I started to feel fatigue again, as if my head were going to fall off of my shoulders. "Carlos, this is so hard for me to say, but I got to say it. I took a pregnancy test."

He slightly jumped and turned his body toward mine. "What, you pregnant, Cook?"

I think thirty seconds passed before I managed to say, "Yes. This is an outcome to some things when we don't use condoms." I was angry at myself when I said that, but I had never used a condom with Carlos and only half of the time I protected myself with Baron. I felt stupider than the dumbest kid in school.

He dropped his head and said, "Pregnant. Damn, I just graduated and now we're pregnant." My eyes almost popped out of my head when he said "we're pregnant."

"Wait, you aren't going to question me about if it's yours or not?"

He turned and looked at me confused, and then, as if a light bulb went off, he said, "That's right. You was having sex with that other nigga."

I didn't even bother to reply.

After a few minutes of the news settling in and Carlos debating within his own mind, he looked up at me and said, "I'm sure it's mine, Cook. I didn't lie when I said I love you. I know I come and go, and I ain't always here, but I'm sure the baby is mine."

I almost wanted to cry. I don't know if it was because of what he said, or the fact that he wasn't angry or denied me. I looked at him and wrapped my arms around his neck. "I just knew I was going to be in this alone."

"Now you know I wouldn't do that. You've been my girl almost my entire life, Cook. I would be the last person to leave you like that. Did you tell Mama?"

I shook my head no. I pushed him playfully and said, "You go tell her, and I'll duck for cover."

"Man, I don't want to tell her. Let's just call her and tell her," he laughed.

"No, 'cause what am I going to do when I go home? She's going to whoop my ass, Carlos. I'm scared," I said playfully, but I was dead serious. I did not want to get a pounding from Della James.

110

He stood up and grabbed my hand and walked me to his car, where he opened his passenger door and told me to get in. "Why? Where are we going? I ain't dressed up to be going anywhere."

"Cook, just get in."

It didn't take me long to realize we were en route to my house. I damn near passed out from fear.

£££

Getting out of the car, Carlos gave me that reassuring nod. I shook my head thinking, *This nigga is about to get beat down and don't even know it.* The front door was open, so I walked on in. Luckily, like always, Lyric wasn't here.

"Mama, are you here?" I yelled out, knowing she was but hoping I got answered by silence.

"Yeah, Cookie, that you or Lyric?" Mama could never tell Lyric's and my voice from one another.

"It's Cook, Ma. Put on some clothes, will ya, and come up to the front. I got to talk to you, and Carlos is here," I managed to say.

"Carlos is here? What y'all want to talk about?"

"Mama, please, just put on some clothes." I had to tell her that Carlos was here, because I could see her walking down the hallway naked. And that is *not* what I want Carlos to remember when he reflected on the day he told my mother I was pregnant.

She walked in dressed in one of her muumuus and took a seat at the table. Carlos walked over to her and gave her a hug. "I know this is not a social visit. I can see Cookie's face over there and know that y'all have done something wrong."

I lowered my head as the anxiety was about to take over my body yet again. Carlos said, "We did want to talk to you, Mama." He

111

took a deep breath, leaned up against the wall across the table, and placed his hands in his pockets.

I sat way across the room on the couch. I glanced up, and Mama was already furious—and we hadn't even told her the news yet. I inched up to the tip of the couch so that I could have a leeway when it was time to run.

"I'm listening," Mama said.

He decided to spread the devastating news of my soon-to-be motherhood. "Mama, I want you to know that I love Cookie; always have since I was nine years old."

"Uh-huh, *and* …?" Mama said. Her deep voice had dropped even more, and I just knew it was time to make a beeline to the front door and quick.

"Cookie and I just found out that she's pregnant."

I think I went deaf at this moment, and I looked up and noticed Mama was already on her feet.

She repeated, "You *pregnant*, Cookie?" Her eyes darted straight toward me as if she was trying to knock the life out of me with them. She was furious, and I couldn't speak.

"Mama, please, I want you to know that I'm going to be here for Cookie and the baby."

I must have blinked slowly because when I looked up, I managed to recognize Mama deep in Carlos's face, yelling—and it wasn't the Christian words she used every Sunday in church.

I sat helpless and felt sorry for Carlos, but when I saw Mama raise her hand and Carlos duck for cover, I jumped up and said, "Mama, don't. I didn't hide this, I didn't go off and just have sex with everyone up under the sun, and it was just Carlos. I do love him."

112

For a minute there I could tell by Mama's reaction that she forgot I was there. That's when she took her first few steps toward me, and I rushed out the front door, slamming the glass window up against the wall.

I could hear Carlos yelling for me and Mama calling me a black this and a black that and slut and all sorts of names. "You ain't supposed to be fucking nobody," I heard her scream.

I was crying terrified tears when I managed to stop and catch my breath. By then, I was a block away from my house. *Oh my God, I left Carlos to fight for himself.* I started to speed walk back toward my street when I saw Carlos's car pull up next to the curb.

"Damn, Cookie, you run fast."

"I put my track experience to use. Did Mama catch you?" I was breathing heavy, trying to catch my breath.

"Yea, but I only managed to get hit a couple times before I got free."

I shook my head in disbelief. Then I started to cry out in agony. I had pain all over. My head, my heart, my stomach, and just about every inch of my body was hurting. I stumbled back, and Carlos jumped out of his car to reach for me.

"Cookie, is you OK?"

"No. I don't feel good at all." Again, my knees felt weak, and I slowly started to fall down. Carlos placed his arms around my waist and walked me over to the passenger-side door. "I'm taking you to JPS."

"I don't want to go to the hospital," I whined.

"You don't have a choice because I'm taking you."

I sat down and pushed his seat all the way back so I could lie down. I felt like crap, and I couldn't wait for the day when this feeling went go away.

£££

When we arrived at the hospital I was escorted to the back to get my vitals taken. The nurse looked at me with concern and asked if I felt OK. I nodded my head that I was fine. I imagined this feeling was from being pregnant. I soon came to know that I was wrong.

My blood pressure was dangerously high, and I was at risk of a seizure. They placed me in a wheelchair and rolled me back to a bed. "How old are you, Ms. James?"

"I'm sixteen," I told the nurse.

She made note of it in her chart and told me to change into the hospital gown. Carlos came in the room five minutes later, and I knew something was wrong because he came to me and started to help me and touch me like I was elderly.

"Carlos, what's going on?"

I noticed that he had an expression of regret; he didn't want to tell me "Your blood pressure is too high, Cookie. I don't think they going to let you go home until it's down. The doctor is coming to see you. I told the nurse that you were pregnant."

I nodded my head that I understood and imagined that they would give me some medicine to bring it down. *It must be due to the stress.* When the doctor came in he brought in a machine and I asked what it was for.

"We're going to take a look at the baby."

I immediately got anxious and nervous at the same time. If the pregnancy test didn't confirm it, this sonogram would.

114

Carlos stood on the opposite side of the doctor and held my hand. He looked more excited than me, and I was happy for him if this made him happy.

"Well, I see the baby's head is already positioned down. Hmmm, that's interesting."

"What, Doctor?" Carlos asked before I could.

"The baby is already in delivery position. How many months did you say you were?"

"I don't know. I just took a test yesterday, but I have honestly been feeling weird for a couple of months now."

"Well, you're definitely more than a couple of months. I'm measuring the baby's head, and I want to say you're somewhere between six–seven months."

I screamed, "What?"

"Yes. You see, you don't look six months yet because you haven't taken any prenatal vitamins."

"I mean, Doc, my stomach is completely flat," I said, lifting up my T-shirt.

"Yes, ma'am, I can see, and the baby is very underweight. I'm going to start you on some prenatal care now and see about getting your blood pressure down. The nurse will be right back in. Now, Ms. James, you lie back and rest on your left side, OK? This is better for the baby."

I nodded my head that I understood and turned over to my left side. I saw Carlos reach for his phone so I asked, "Who are you calling?"

"My mama. She's going to want to know about this."

"Fine. While you're at it, call my mama and Sierra. If something is wrong with me, then I want them to know."

The End Of The Road

I looked at the food the nurse had given me and wanted to puke. I was tired of this low-sodium diet they had me on. In three weeks, I had gained thirty pounds, my belly had ballooned to the fact where you *knew* I was seven months, and my blood pressure stayed dangerously high. I was not going home until I had this baby. *Had this baby. I still couldn't believe I was pregnant. I had only just turned sixteen.*

Every day I was bored, miserable, and depressed. Carlos came up daily, but he didn't have to stay in this hellhole. I did. Sierra would spend evenings with me after she got out of school, because now I was missing the beginning of my junior year.

Today wasn't any different. I woke up at six a.m. to get my vitals from the nurse, who, in turn, told me again my pressure was still high, gave me a snack, and left me to be alone. Then Lyric knocked on my hospital door.

"Hey, sis, are you up?" she asked.

"What are you doing here?"

"I didn't have to go into work today and decided to come and check in on you."

"Oh yeah, and what else?" I knew she had to be coming for other reasons. Don't get me wrong. We were sisters, but just because we got older and didn't fight anymore didn't mean we didn't have our differences. I loved her because she was my sister, not because she was a good person.

116

"Johnny gets out today. I'm coming to see him, and you know, move on."

The sound of Johnny's name made me think of Baron. I hadn't been able to visit him in weeks due to be being on the third floor of the same hospital he was in.

"So Johnny's leaving?"

"Yea. Have you been able to go up and see Baron? He's on the fifth floor now and doing good in rehab."

"No, but I sure want to. Is he up and talking?"

"Yep." Lyric poked her head out the door to see if anyone was coming. "I'm going to tell the nurses I'm taking you outside for some air for ten minutes seeing as though you haven't been outside in almost a month."

"OK, but where are you really taking me?"

"To see Baron."

"Oh my God, I can't do that. He doesn't know I'm pregnant, and look at me. I'm all fat and ugly, and my hair ain't done." Lyric walked up to me and proceeded to brush my hair that was actually naps now.

"You are gonna be fine, Cook. You got to go see him."

I took a deep breath and allowed myself to prepare to see Baron for the first time in weeks. I didn't know what he would say when he noticed I was pregnant—and seven months pregnant at that.

£££

The ride up the elevator was nerve-racking. I had a blanket over my legs to keep them warm and was wearing my favorite pink fuzzy socks. Once we got to the floor, Lyric rolled me to his room door. I told her to wait outside and that I had it from here.

117

Wrapping my hands around the wheels of my chair, I pushed myself through the doorway and noticed his attention was on the television. I tapped lightly on the door and called out, "Baron!"

When he turned his head, I could see the swelling had gone down; he looked almost like he used to except for a little discoloration and scars. "Cookie?" he asked as if he were confused. Maybe he didn't recognize me under all of this fat.

"Yes, it's me." I rolled closer to his bed, but not too close. I was too embarrassed of the way I was looking.

He sat up slowly not taking his eyes off of me. His eyes trailed up and down, taking in the fact that I too was in a hospital gown. "What happened to you? Where have you been?"

"I've been on the third floor of this hospital for the passed three-and-a-half weeks. Before that, I used to come see you in the ICU almost every day, hoping I'd get a moment to talk to you again, and here you are." I almost wanted to cry noticing for the first time in months I was speaking to him.

"You're in the hospital too? Did something happen to you that night? I've been asking my family to reach out to you, but they said they couldn't find you."

I lowered my head and prepared myself to stand up. I wasn't allowed to stand or sit up, for that matter, due to my blood pressure. But showing him I was pregnant verses telling him was better in my book. I took my first step and dropped the blanket away from my body.

"Are you pregnant?"

"Yes, I'm seven months now. I've been in the hospital because I have had problems with my blood pressure, and I'm at risk of going into premature labor and having a seizure."

118

He reached his hand out motioning he wanted to touch my belly. Slowly, I walked over to him, and I felt a shock of electricity shoot through my body when his hand connected with my stomach. I jumped a little and smiled.

"Yeah, I felt that too." He rubbed his hand over my stomach in a circular motion and said, "I'm going to be a daddy?"

My heart dropped. I never once thought about Baron being the father after I told Carlos. It was like Baron didn't exist, but who was I fooling? Baron was a great guy. He felt something for me to have risked his life for me, and here I was planning a life with someone who was always in and out of my life. I stood there and thought he very well could be the father too.

I couldn't tell him that he probably wasn't. I couldn't bring up Carlos now. It would have to be when I was out of the hospital and Baron was a lot better.

I just nodded my head and smiled.

He said, "I got to hurry up and get out of here. You said you're seven months. Kind of works out. They say I'll be out of here within a couple weeks, hopefully. I can get a job and a place for us to stay. It's going to all work out, Cookie, I promise."

I reached over toward his table and grabbed the ballpoint pen and paper and wrote down my room's phone number. "Here. Let's get on the phone and talk and you can keep me posted on your recovery. I can't leave my room. This is my first time leaving in almost a month."

"OK. Maybe I can get my physical therapist to take me down there to see you too. Write your room number down."

I did and leaned down to give him a hug and a kiss on the cheek. I whispered in his ear, "Thank you for being there for me," and

119

got back into my wheelchair and rolled away. I was glad to have talked to him, but this baby situation didn't make things easier. I didn't know who the father was.

£££

Only a week had passed since my encounter with Baron, and the nurse was reading over my test results from the sonogram. The baby hadn't moved enough in the time required.

"What does that mean, Nurse?"

"Latoya, your pressure is pretty high today, and the baby isn't showing enough activity. I'm going to show this to the doctor, and then he'll decide what to do."

I didn't really believe the doctor when I heard him say, "Move her to the Labor and Delivery unit." I thought perhaps they'll just monitor me over there more closely. I picked up my phone before the nurse could wheel me out and called Carlos.

"Hey, I don't know what's going on, but they're moving me to Labor and Delivery."

"Labor and Delivery! Is you in labor?"

"No, but they say the baby hasn't moved much and that my pressure is too high. I guess they want to watch me over there closely or something." He said he would be right up after calling Mama.

My room was beautiful and spacious and even had a separate couch for family.

Oh, I've moved on up in the world. I'm going to like staying over here.

The nurse helped me out of my wheelchair and said, "Ms. James, you do know that we are inducing your labor, right?"

"What's inducing?" I said, shrugging my shoulders.

"The baby is in distress and too much pressure is on her. We have to deliver her tonight."

The nurse had to repeat the words. I can only imagine what my reaction was like, because for the first time since discovering I was pregnant, I knew that I was about to have a baby and that there was no going back.

"The baby is coming *tonight?*"

"Yes, ma'am. Now please, lie back so I can hook you up to the monitor. In about thirty minutes I will be in here with the doctors and we are going to break your water."

"Break it?"

"Yes, we will rupture the sack the baby is in and the fluids will pour out. It will feel like you peed on yourself." I nodded my head and tried to take in everything she was telling me.

I don't think I'm ready for this.

I lay back on the bed and watched the nurse hook me up to the different monitors, and like clockwork, two other nurses and a doctor came in to break my water. I was about to go through some pure hell.

I closed my eyes and started to think of who I should talk to. I hadn't prayed to God in ages. Wonder if he would remember who I was at this moment. I've heard of women dying in labor, and I surely don't want to go to hell for not talking to him all this time. Maybe if I'd just be honest, he'll understand. I mean it's God. He understands anyway.

OK, Lord, you know it's me, Cookie. Oh yeah, wait, I need to use my real name. It's me, Latoya. So I kind of messed up and had sex with Baron a few months ago, then turned around and started having sex with Carlos. Now I know that was wrong, but it was hard to resist, you know. Especially hanging around Lyric and Lynn. I know after

121

Sierra being raped I shouldn't have been thinking about sex, but I had my own mind. Anyway, I wanted to talk to you for a minute. These doctors say I'm about to have this baby, a person I've only known about for two months or so, and I want to make sure she's all right. She's going to be little and probably sick, and I don't want her to suffer because of me. Even Mama has come around and is embracing her, and she has got to make it. I don't care what I have to do in life; I just want her to be OK.

Now I can feel them sticking that stick up me, Lord, to break my water. Can you please watch over me? I don't want to die. At least not right now. I know I used to tell you I wanted to die all those years ago, but it's different now. I have this baby, and Mama is sick. She can't take care of a child by herself. I'll go back to who I used to be and stop hanging around Lyric if you let me be OK. Lord, I feel the water coming out this time. Please, please, please, watch over me and my baby. I'm going to name her Daijah. I know you've met her already, but if you can give me the chance to be a great mother, I'm sure I won't let you down.

Remember, Lord, I love you. Always have and always will. I'm going to lie back now and allow you to take over my body. I'm starting to feel a slight pain now. Might be that contraction thing they mentioned. I'm going to have faith in you and believe that in the end we will all be OK. I love you.

Tamika Newhouse

You Are Not The Father

I stood looking in the mirror with Sierra sitting on my bed watching me, shaking her head and laughing. I was enjoying this moment too, because I was back to my bona fide body. I was sexy as hell, and my hips were just the right fullness. Daijah did me a favor after all.

"I can't believe how fine you are, slut. It's only been two weeks since you dropped that baby."

"Aw, Sierra, poo; don't hate on me; hate on Mother Nature," I laughed out.

"Are you ready to go? Carlos has been waiting on us for a while now, and I know he and Mama will be distracted and start playing dominoes or something. So let's go."

I shut off my room lights and walked into the living room. Carlos was eating a slice of Mama's tuna sandwich. She looked up and noticed me coming in. "Heifer, don't go back out there being fast now that you got your shape back," Mama said.

Carlos eyed me with a little too much intensity. I knew he hated the fact that my hips were definitely like Nia Long's, and let's not forget my butt now was a ripe apple. I shrugged my shoulders and went ahead and grabbed a sandwich myself.

"Mama, we'll be back in a few. I want to be in the NICU with Daijah for at least two hours this time. I think they may let her come home next week."

Daijah was immediately taken to the NICU due to being underweight, and she needed constant attention. But in a matter of two weeks, she was gaining weight and was almost strong enough to feed from a bottle.

Bad thing is, during this time, I had been avoiding Baron, who was now out of the hospital. I tried to block out the future confrontation I would have because I knew at some point I was going to have to tell him. Lyric let me know that he was upset about me having the baby and not telling him, and that he didn't understand why. How was I going to tell him that he wasn't the father?

I was certain he wasn't because like night and day, Daijah looked just like Carlos. I breathed a sigh of relief every day that I looked at her; she barely even looked like me. She had his mouth, nose, eyes, hairline; everything screamed Carlos. And everyone who saw the baby said the same thing.

I hopped in Carlos's car with Sierra in tow, and we rode up to John Peter Smith to see my little angel, the one I couldn't wait to bring home.

£££

It was only a matter of days and Daijah would be home. With Lyric moved out into her own apartment, I wasted no time redecorating her room. One day, Carlos surprised me and came by the house and handed me $400 and said go buy whatever the baby needed. I anxiously got Mama to take me to Wal-Mart, buying diapers, wipes, baby clothes, bottles, a crib, a bouncer, and baby products to bath her with. This was the start I needed to be ready for her to come home. Not to mention some of Mama's friends gave us some old clothes and one of my aunt's got me a stroller. I was almost set.

Back at the house I was unpacking everything I bought and organizing her room to the very smallest of details, taking all of my old

125

bears and stuffed animals and placing them along the walls on the floor. I heard Mama yell my name from the living room, telling me that I had a phone call.

Racing to the receiver, I placed it to my ear and said, "Hello."

"Oh. so you're available now," I heard Baron say. He was upset, almost to the point of yelling. I glanced up at Mama to see if she could hear his outburst. She eyed me, and I could tell she was thinking, *Who the hell is that?*

Ducking down the hallway and closing my bedroom door I whispered, "Baron, I can't talk right now."

"What do you mean you can't talk right now? I heard you had our baby, and you haven't even called me. That's messed up, Cook. What's up with you?"

"I wanted to talk to you in person, Baron, but it's not been a good time for me, plus with getting out of the hospital I'm trying to rest. But ..."

"But what?"

"Look, Baron, I'm not certain. I mean, look, do we have to have this conversation over the phone?"

"Apparently so, because I don't know where the hell you live."

"OK, Baron, watch your tone with me. I know I'm wrong for not calling you or telling you about Daijah."

"You named her Daijah? It's a girl."

The more Baron talked, the worse I felt. I had to tell him now and not prolong this. "Baron, she isn't yours. This is why I haven't called. I didn't know how to tell you."

"What did you just say?"

126

"I thought she was, but she isn't, and I'm sorry, Baron. You know how I feel about you. And how you were there for me that night, and you risked your life for me, but I can't control this outcome. Daijah isn't yours."

"I can't believe you just said that to me."

I fell silent waiting for him to reply, but when the line went dead I breathed a sigh of relief. But I wanted to know how he was doing. Was he upset or was he relieved? Did I break his heart?

I plopped down on my bed looking up at the ceiling thinking about how much things had changed. I was a mother at sixteen, and damn near was going to miss half of my junior year.

I started to wipe away the tears that escaped my eyes. I didn't know if I was sad, happy, or mad. My family had judged me; Lola wouldn't even take my phone calls because she called herself being disappointed in me; and although Mama loves Daijah, she hates the fact that I got pregnant, which is contradictory, to me anyhow.

And although I didn't care what my classmates thought, I didn't want to be known as a ho because I had a baby. It would be interesting to see how my classmates reacted anyhow, since I never walked the halls of my high school with a pregnant belly. So no one really knew.

Life isn't going to be that hard, Cook; you can do this. I started to think about Carlos and how he has been there, but how he can walk away at any moment. I was the one stuck. I was the mama. The baby stayed with me. He has continuously asked for Daijah to spend half the time with him when she gets home, but I could never trust myself around his family, who I didn't know.

127

I just felt that life wasn't about selling stolen checks to get a quick buck, stealing clothes from Old Navy, smoking weed, or having sex with my boyfriend with his mama in the next room anymore. Life was more than that. I had to think about someone else before my own self this time around. I was no longer just a girl. I was a mother.

Tamika Newhouse

TWO YEARS LATER

Time Doesn't Stand Still

I swear I felt as if the world were watching me at this moment. I tried to relax and breathe in deeply. No one could see me anyhow. I was in the back of the grocery store in the section that I needed most. At home I had counted that Daijah had two diapers left, and I was tired of asking Mama for help so that I could get things I needed for the baby. Just last week I had run out of food for her, and thank God she wasn't on any milk anymore because I wouldn't be able to get her that.

I poked my head around the corner to see if a worker was coming, and the coast was clear. Quickly, I opened my backpack and ripped open a bag of diapers. Adrenaline rushed through my veins as I heisted Pampers in hopes of not getting caught. Once I was satisfied with the amount I had stolen, I zipped up my bag and proceeded to walk out of the store.

This will last me until next week when I get my check from Julie's Kitchen. It was a hot day in March as I made my way back to Mama's car. We had gotten rid of the van a year ago. I threw my bag in the back and turned the ignition on. Looking back, I backed out of the parking spot to make the short ride back home. I thought about making a trip to Sierra's, but I knew she was probably at work. I tried to block the fact that I had just stolen Pampers so that my baby wouldn't go without.

I needed to get in the house and bath Daijah and get to bed early anyhow with morning classes tomorrow and work right after. I knew I wasn't going to be hitting my bed again till well after ten o'clock tomorrow night. It was eight now, so I decided to go ahead and get a head start.

Walking in, I could hear Mama and Daijah in the back watching TV. I went into the kitchen to make sure the chicken I had cooked was done. It was. I cut off all the burners and yelled out and told Mama the food was ready. I decided to make her and Daijah a plate before I went and got Daijah's things ready for day care tomorrow.

After setting up the stolen pampers in Daijah's room, I walked into my bedroom, picking up my cell phone I left on my bed. I glanced at its screen and it read no missed calls. *Of course, Carlos hasn't called. Probably out with his friends again as usual.* Then I heard the patter of little feet running toward my room before I saw her and looked up.

"Daijah, are you done eating? Your hands are dirty." I raced toward her and grabbed her hands before she could touch anything, leading her to the bathroom. I decided to go ahead and run her bathwater and bathe her while I was at it.

"Cookie, has you heard from Lyric?" I shrugged my shoulders and yelled no to Mama even before she could finish the question. Lyric ran through here like a blue moon. Once she moved that was it. She doesn't bother to come see us every day, only when she wanted to come and get Daijah, which was about once a week or so.

"Why? Do you need me to call her or something?" I yelled back, pulling Daijah out of the water and wrapping a towel around her.

"I need to borrow some money from her."

"How much you need, Mama?"

131

"Just some gas money and something to buy food with."

I breathed out in aggravation again. Mama had stopped working completely at this point because she was too sick. Her diabetes had taken a turn for the worse, and she could barely walk due to her excessive weight.

I started to jog through my memory and remembered I had fifty dollars put up from my last check. I waitressed at Julie's Kitchen, which was right up the street. It was enough money to pay for Daijah's everyday things and help Mama some around the house. After all the bills, I would make $100 spread for an entire month.

"I have a little something, Mama; you know Lyric is going to say she ain't got it. Which is probably a lie because you know she be writing them checks."

Lyric, who had moved out a couple of years ago, was with a guy we knew was on drugs. She started dating him after she and Johnny broke up. But since she started with him, she got into all sorts of illegal messes, and even got Kyra and one of her other friends involved in writing hot checks. She stole a few of Mama's checks and since then, we had to hide everything from her as if she were a crackhead.

"That's OK; I'll call Lola and see what she can send us. Hold your money because you got to pay for your senior pictures."

I sucked my teeth in anger, forgetting I had to pay for my pictures this week. I needed to pay for some college applications too and was behind on that. Laying my daughter down on the bed to dry her off, I was contemplating finding another job.

I was grateful I had day care assistance through the county, but they wouldn't give us food stamps, saying Mama's SSI money was

132

enough. We lived off of less than $1,200 a month, and with Daijah, rent, bills, the car note, and my senior expenses, we were barely making it. Lyric came through every now and then to give Mama some money, but she would talk bad to her so much I told her to stay the hell away. I hated when she disrespected Mama for no reason but bent over backward for her drug-dealing boyfriend.

"I'll call Carlos and see if he's coming this week with some money." *I need to put his ass on child support.* I was with Carlos, but then again, he came by about four times a week for about an hour a day. He just looked at and played with Daijah then left. Just enough time for me to barely catch a nap. He gave us money every week but sometimes that was after he paid for whatever he wanted. So I got the sloppy seconds. Other times he would come over when he wanted to have sex. And most of the time I had sex because not only did it feel good, but I loved it when he was around.

When I thought about what my life used to be like and what it was now, I was living the life of a thirty-year-old. I didn't have a social life, barely any friends, and I had a baby. I imagined Daijah was a blessing, but in the end, I felt like I was being punished for a blessing I didn't necessarily want.

Once A Good Girl Goes Bad She's Gone Forever

One thing I enjoyed about my senior year was I got out of school at eleven in the morning. I didn't bother to stay around to socialize with my classmates or participate in the senior activities because, to be honest, I already felt like an adult. I was living my life already. As I was hopping in Mama's car, my cell phone rang. It was Lyric's number.

"Are you out of school?" I heard Lynn yell through the phone.

"Yea, what's up?"

"Come get your sister. Renzel and she are in a fight again. They busted holes in the wall, and she's threatening to kill him with a knife."

Oh, she still playing the butcher woman; first me, and now this nigga.

"I'm on my way." Shaking my head in annoyance, I did a U-turn and made a beeline to Lyric's apartment. She stayed a couple blocks away from my school. Pulling up into the complex I was always mistaken that I was on the Southside in the hood. These were some of the worst apartments in our predominately white neighborhood.

When I drove around to where she stayed, I started to cuss under my breath when I heard them yelling and screaming. *If this ain't some ghetto mess here.* I looked up and saw Renzel out by her car, and Lyric stood on her balcony and threw a glass at him. It shattered only inches away from him. I hurried and parked and got out.

"Yo', Lyric, what the hell is going on?"

134

"I'm going to kill him, Cook. He's having sex with the girl who stays right under me," she screamed. At least that's what I thought she said. She had gained about thirty pounds and was huffing and puffing as each word came out of her mouth. I noticed Lynn walk up to me. She wanted a ride home.

I told her to go wait in the car. I walked up the stairs into Lyric's trashed apartment and yelled, "Why the hell do you choose to live like this? Look at this mess."

"I just ain't cleaned today, that's all." Her hair was all of over her head, and you could even see some hair glue stuck to her scalp. Her clothes were torn, and I imagined it was from fighting with Renzel. One thing Lyric did was fight a nigga like she was a man. I didn't like Renzel. One, he wasn't educated; two, he sold drugs; three, he cheated all the time; four, he lived off of my sister; five, he was a crackhead. I didn't have proof, but I knew he was. You don't drop weight that quickly and look sick in the face if it wasn't drugs. I had several cousins and uncles who were on drugs, and when Mama pointed this out about Renzel, I knew he was a crackhead too.

I walked over thrown pillows, a knocked down TV, garbage, and movie discs, and followed her to her room which was just as bad, and it didn't help that her room stunk. "What the hell is that smell?" I squeezed my nose to try to hide the funk.

She started to ramble off about how she was breaking up with him. I had honestly heard this from the time she got with him two years ago. It was the same ole sad love song. "Lyric, I'm about to take Lynn home, and then I'll be back. Try to clean up this mess. Where is Renzel going?"

"Tell him to go to hell."

Shaking my head, I walked back out toward the parking lot and saw Renzel yelling to someone on his phone, "Renzel, is you all right?" It wasn't like I cared. I just wanted to know where he was going.

"Yea, Cook, I'm gonna have my nigga come and get me. Yo' sister is crazy."

Opening up my driver-side door, I said, "Yes, she is, but go ahead and leave tonight and call tomorrow or something after she cools down. I'm out."

Lynn said, "Girl, get me outta this damn zoo."

I laughed and placed the car in reverse to take her home.

£££

After dropping Lynn off, I glanced at my phone to see if I had any missed calls, and I had none. I wasn't surprised either. Days would go by before Carlos would call. Then he would just pop by the house. I knew he was content with knowing I was always at home with our baby, staying faithful, and doing nothing. But I had made a conscious decision that, even though I had a child, my life wasn't over. I was going to go out and have fun too.

I opened up my phone seeing that it was after one to check in on Mama. "Hey, Mama, you need anything?"

"No, I'm OK. Where are you at?"

I lied and said I was at the library filling out my applications. Which is where I should have been instead of being at Lyric's, and then Lynn Shaffer's. I didn't want her to be bothered with yet another Lyric story.

"I'm on my way to Sierra's now; she should be home about this time. I'll pick up Daijah, and then we'll be on our way home." She

136

said OK, and then we hung up. I dialed Sierra's number to make sure she was at home.

"Hey, heifer, where are you?" I heard her say. She was becoming more and more like my idol. She was at the top of our class, had an acceptance letter from Howard, and was casually dating a college guy she met a few months ago. She was living the life I wish I had. I would be sad to see her leave for Washington, D.C., after this summer passed.

"Are you at home? I wanted to stop by."

"Yeah, come on by. I was about to put a pizza in the oven. I'm hungry as hell. Bring some sodas, will ya?" I said OK and hung up.

After all the drama with me being pregnant, and then not hanging out with Lyric anymore, I have only one friend, and Sierra was the last person standing. As I was pulling up into the parking lot my phone rang. I looked at the screen and noticed it was Carlos. *Oh, how lucky am I to get a call today!*

"Yes," I answered, not wanting to seem too happy to hear him. I was more annoyed about the little time he gave Daijah and me, which wasn't much.

"Hey, babe, where are you at?"

"I'm out about to meet Sierra. What's up?"

"Why does it seem you're rushing me off the phone?"

I rolled my eyes in annoyance. "Sorry you feel that way. I'm simply about to go hang out with my friend, and you called at a bad time. Funny thing is that you even called," I sarcastically said.

"Here we go again."

"No, this conversation isn't going anywhere really. Because like I said, I'm busy and Sierra wants to take me out tonight."

137

"Out where? Where will our daughter be while you're out?" He was clearly annoyed with the idea of me not being at home.

"She'll be with my mother or my aunt around the corner—wait—unless you want to actually come and see our child. That would be great. Go pick her up from day care."

"Go pick her up?"

"Yea, sure, why not?"

"You never let me take her anywhere. Now you want to me to come pick her up? Why? Who are you going out with?"

I started to laugh, and my grin was from ear to ear as my plan to make him jealous worked. I said, "Sierra. I'll call Mama and let her know Daijah is with you."

"Wait a minute now, I didn't say I was going."

"Are you telling me that for the first time when I allow you to get our child you're saying no?" He started to stutter. "I didn't think so. I'll call you tonight. Make sure to get her by four, please." I hung up without saying good-bye. I had another plan. Sierra was going to take me out to the ballroom. It was a Friday night and instead of sitting by my phone, I was going to go out and have some fun for a change.

£££

After begging Sierra to let me wear her new denim jeans and black halter top that stopped right above my navel, we were ready to go. I was excited about going out and Sierra didn't hesitate to take me out. She missed us hanging out.

We hopped in her new Chevy Cavalier and headed on 35 South to the ballroom, which most teens in Fort Worth went to on the weekends. I reached in my purse, pulled out a twenty and my ID.

"Girl, put that money up. I know you on a tight budget. I got you tonight. And when we leave, we can hit up the Waffle House right around the corner." I gladly dropped my money back into my purse.

It was a little after nine when we made our hike up to the front door. The bouncer examined us and waved the metal detector over our bodies, then let us in. I headed straight for the bar area to order a Sprite.

The room was dark, and the music was blasting. The disco ball in the middle of the dance floor had the room sparkling with different colors of silver and purple. I took my drink from the guy behind the counter and downed it. Its hard citrus taste caused me to gasp for air. Suddenly, I felt a pat on my back and a male say, "You drinking that like it's water."

Coughing, I took my hand and wiped the tears from my eyes that had formed. "Yeah, just a little nervous. I haven't been here before." I turned and glanced to see who I was talking to, and my eyes caught the face of a beautiful brotha. And I do mean beautiful. Well, to me, that is. He had hazel eyes, a mocha-brown complexion, was tall, with pretty teeth. I had to look around and make sure he was talking to me.

"So you don't get out much?" he asked.

Assuming he saw my uncertainty I said, "No. I work and go to go school, you know?"

"Oh, a good girl. I like that. Want me to buy you another soda? Perhaps some wings too?"

I nodded my head yes. I wasn't going to turn down free food. I followed him to a sitting area, glancing around to find Sierra, who was already dancing with a guy on the dance floor.

"Is that your friend?" he asked, catching my eyes on Sierra.

139

"Yeah, my best friend. Do you come here a lot?"

"Nope. I play ball at Dunbar, so I'm either studying for the SAT or practicing."

"So you're a senior too?"

"Yea, what school do you go to?" he asked.

"Hills High."

"Oh yea? My friend had a cousin who went there. His name was Trent, but he got killed a couple years ago."

I flinched when he said Trent's name and flashbacked to that day at Gateway Park.

"Are you OK?"

"Oh yeah, I'm sorry. I knew Trent. He was a good friend of mine, and I blocked that pain out of my head, you know, to get past it."

"Oh, I'm sorry. Let's change the subject. I didn't introduce myself. I'm Patrick, and you are?"

"Cookie."

He smiled and I looked at him bashfully and asked him what he was smiling at.

"The name Cookie fits you. Dark chocolate skin can be mistaken for something edible."

I rolled my eyes and gave him a slight push on his shoulder. "Trying to talk some *game* to me, I see."

He laughed and said, "Before our wings get here, how about a dance? I like this song."

"Four Page Letter" by Aaliyah was playing, and I guess I couldn't resist. I took his hand and followed him to the dance floor. I was happy to see that he stood taller than me. He could have been about six feet to my five seven. I wrapped my arms around his neck and leaned in, making sure to allow him to lead me in the direction I should go. Ironically, I closed my eyes and allowed myself to not think about what I was doing. He would find out sooner or later anyway that I couldn't dance worth a dime.

£££

I found myself sitting at a booth with Patrick, Sierra, and a new friend of hers named Drew. It was starting to get well after midnight when I glanced at my phone. I felt like the world had closed in on me when I realized I hadn't checked in on Daijah. Quickly, I stepped away from the table and went into the bathroom to make my much-needed phone call. I noticed a missed call from Mama an hour ago and dialed her back.

"Hey, Mama, are you still up?"

"Where the hell are you at?" She was asleep, and her voice sounded groggy.

"I'm sorry I forgot to call. Sierra took me to the ballroom. That's where I am now."

"Is that a club? Why the hell you at a club?"

"I just wanted to go out and have fun. It's not really a club; it's a place teens go to dance and stuff. I go to school, work, and take care of Daijah every day; I just wanted a chance to finally have fun."

"Hmmm, I guess so, huh. Carlos has been calling here every hour on the hour asking if you were home since you ain't answering your cell."

"I can't hear it with all this music though, and plus, I don't feel like talking to him."

"Oh, really now? And why is that? You're just getting a little too grown for me."

"Mama, when I got pregnant I took that responsibility. I don't go out, I'm passing my classes, I pay bills, I take care of home, and I got a job. Yeah, Carlos calls himself loving me and Daijah, but he ain't there to do all the work. I am. The little time he spends ain't enough, and I'm not going to sit around waiting for his call or his visits."

"Did you tell him that?"

"Yes."

"All right, Cookie, you make your decisions. You right, you have done all of those things and without much complaint to me. I know I hated the fact you got pregnant at sixteen, but I am proud of the woman you have become. Just don't do anything you will regret."

"I'll be home in a couple hours, Mama. Love ya. And I won't." I hung up the phone and noticed several missed calls from Carlos. I decided to shoot him a text, that I'll be over to get Daijah tomorrow. And then I turned my phone off.

Making my way back toward the table, I saw Sierra get up from the table and announce we were all about to leave. I glanced toward Patrick who said he was coming with us.

"Where're we going?"

"To the Waffle House. You know I'm hungry, girl," Sierra said. I nodded my head and followed her to her car. We hopped in, and Sierra wasted no time interrogating me about Patrick.

"So I see Patrick and you are really feeling each other," she laughed.

"Yea, he's cool." I didn't want to seem too excited, but I was excited to have some attention from someone new.

"He plays ball too, huh? Good catch, Cook."

"Who said I was trying to go there with him?"

"He says it. I can see it all over his face. Look, I know you digging Carlos still and you love him and all that, but sis, you are seventeen. That nigga be in and out and don't even take you out. You too young for that mess. Have fun. I won't tell." She laughed again making her way in the Waffle House parking lot.

Instead of replying, I hopped out of the car when she parked to meet Patrick by the front door. I decided to just let tonight be a fun night and not think about it too much and see where it went. We took a booth next to the window facing the highway and proceeded to glance over the menu.

No need to decide what I wanted because the All-Star breakfast was already on my mind. I could sense Patrick staring at me as he asked me what I was going to eat.

I shyly replied making sure to miss his eye contact. There was something about him that gave me that puppy-love-crush syndrome.

I was lost in a trance when I heard a familiar voice say, "It's been a minute, Cook." I glanced up and had to blink twice when I saw Baron.

It had been two years since I had last seen him, which was in the hospital after he got shot. His discovery of Daijah not being his caused us to never speak again—that is, until right now. I sometimes imagined if I would feel this alone in a relationship if he were Daijah's father. But I would always quickly erase that thought, because truth was, he wasn't.

"Baron, oh my God. How have you been?" I slid out of the booth, telling Patrick I would be right back. Seeing Baron took my breath away, and I could sense Sierra eyeballing me, questioning how I was going to handle this situation.

143

"I'm doing good. Look at you. All grown up." It was true; I had grown in the past two years, cutting my hair in the process and gaining about twenty pounds but in all the right places.

"Yeah, I have, and look at you." I couldn't get past his facial hair, his broad shoulders, the fact that he obviously worked out, and his hair was cut into a low fade. I had to remind myself to blink.

He reached in and gestured for a hug, and I accepted. He smelled good too. I counted in my head and guessed he was around twenty-two years old now. I still couldn't believe that I was standing here talking to him.

"So what are you doing out here?" I asked.

"We just came from Club Jamie's. I stay on this side of town and decided to get something to eat before I went home." He glanced at the table and said, "Is that your man? I don't want to be disrespectful."

"No, I just met him tonight. Are you by yourself?" I said, looking around over his shoulder to see if anyone was waiting on him.

"Yea, I was just gonna get some takeout." An uncomfortable thirty seconds passed before he said, "Here, take my number. Call me when you get in tonight."

"Tonight? Are you sure?"

"Cookie, I've waited two years to see you again. Yeah, I'm sure." He leaned in after giving me his number on a torn piece of paper and gave me a hug. I hugged him back and closed my eyes to try to remember how it felt to be held by him again.

We said our good-byes and I seriously did not want to just walk away, but I didn't want to be rude to Patrick either. *He wants me to call him tonight. I wonder about what.*

After sitting down at the table I turned my phone on and disregarded the texts from Carlos and shot Sierra a message to her phone. I wanted to get out of Waffle House as soon as I could to call the one person I felt I would never stop caring for. I mean, you always feel something for your very first, right?

£££

I made sure to open the door as quietly as I could as I made my way back into the house at almost three in the morning. I could hear Mama snoring even before I opened the door. I jogged to the kitchen to get the cordless phone and started to dial in Baron's number. Taking off my shoes and shirt, I walked back to my room as the phone rang.

"Hello," I heard him say.

"You didn't go to sleep on me, did you?"

"Of course not. I haven't been able to close my eyes since I seen you an hour ago. Can you talk?"

"Yeah, I just got into my room now and closed my door. It's just me and you."

"Oh yeah, just me and you, huh?"

"You sound the same," I giggled, remembering how his voice used to sound.

"You don't. When I saw you tonight I just knew I was tripping. I figured my eyes were playing tricks on me, but nope, it was you. Sitting there smiling and laughing. You have that same beautiful smile, you know."

"Baron, stop. You're making me blush."

"You've grown up, Cook, into a beautiful woman. I'm glad I saw you tonight."

145

Cookie

"Same here. Two years is a long time, you know? I figured you would have hated me. You still cross my mind from time to time."

"Oh, yeah? And what do you be thinking about?" he laughed.

"Ugh. Come on, don't make me say it."

"Come on, tell me."

"Well, I always wondered if you went off to college or if you had kids now and if you still stayed with your mama. Stuff like that," I laughed. I tried to stop from smiling because my cheeks were starting to hurt, but I couldn't. Talking to Baron again made all of my old feelings resurface.

"Well, I go to the county college, I don't stay with my mama, and I have a one-year-old son."

"A son, huh?"

"Yeah, he's a junior. How about you, Cook? How's the baby?"

I reluctantly replied remembering how Baron was upset to find out he wasn't the father of Daijah. "I'm good. I work now, go to school, and you know, about to graduate. I plan on doing the county college thing and transferring to the university in two years. I stay with Mama. Just me and Daijah."

He paused for a few seconds before he said, "How about we meet up next weekend? I bring my son, and you bring Daijah."

"As in a date?"

"We don't have to call it that, but something like that."

I thought about the last time I was on a date. At the age of seventeen and having a child so young I haven't had my fair share of dates. And don't let me get started on the lack of quality time Carlos

146

was giving. I mean, what the heck? It was only a date, right? The kids would be with us anyhow.

"OK, yeah. I can do that."

£££

I looked out my bedroom window to see who had pulled up, and lo and behold, I see Lyric's car. I hadn't seen her come by the house in two weeks since I let her borrow my last twenty bucks. And right about now, I was needing that for gas for the week.

I didn't bother to get up out of my bed as I heard her enter the house, and I rolled my eyes when I heard Renzel's voice trail in behind her.

I could hear her yell out, "Come here, fat mama," as she scooped Daijah into her arms. I rolled my eyes at how she annoyed me. I rolled off of my bed and made my way into the living room anyway to ask for my money. I glanced into Mama's room and saw her getting into her wheelchair.

Over the passed several months, Mama's body began to weaken to the point of where I had to help her move around the house. She couldn't cook anymore or bathe herself, so I spent most of my time doing what needed to be done around the house.

I yelled toward her, "Are you coming up to the living room?"

Placing her legs in front of her she nodded her head yes. I proceeded to make my way down to the living room. "So what are y'all doing over here?"

"Just came to check on y'all and see what's up. Did you cook?" She smelled the pork chops I had baking in the oven and cabbage I had simmering in a skillet.

"Yeah, I cooked for us." I gave Renzel a weak head nod to acknowledge his presence and took a seat on the couch.

I turned when I heard Mama's electric wheelchair zoom down the hallway. Daijah ran up to her trying to catch a ride as if it were a toy.

"Dang, we can't get a sample of the food?" Lyric complained when I told her that the food was not for her and Renzel.

Renzel walked up to Mama to give her a hug. I always felt like he kissed her ass so we wouldn't state the obvious of his drug-addictive ways.

"No, you can't have any. I got to make that stretch for tomorrow. Did you bring my money, by the way?"

"What money?"

"The twenty I let you hold over a week ago. I need that back for gas this week."

"Oh, here you go li'l sis," Renzel said, pulling out a ball of money wrapped up by a rubber band.

"Well, since you in the giving mood, can you let me have another thirty?" I glanced at Mama and winked, not wanting to break a smile.

Lyric protested and said, "For what?"

"Well, I need some co-pay money to get Mama's insulin; you know, the medicine that help keeps her alive." I rolled my eyes at her and turned my attention back to Renzel. I could tell he didn't want to part with his thirty bucks, but who would say no to that. I was laughing inside because truth be told, I just needed it for the water bill. But if I would have said that I probably wouldn't have gotten it. I took the money, folded it, and placed it in my bra.

I left Mama to talk to them, and she played a game of dominoes with Renzel. After two hours or so, Lyric was on her way again. I didn't waste any time getting Daijah in the tub and to bed because after meeting Baron for our double date with our kids last week, I had a one-on-one date with him tonight and didn't want any interruptions.

While searching for some clothes in my closet I heard my phone ring. Looking at the caller ID, I prepared myself for an interrogation.

"Hey, what's up?"

"Hey, yourself. I haven't heard from you since two days ago." If I didn't have an alternative motive I would praise myself for this chain of events. Carlos was now calling me. He saw the difference in my attitude toward him. I guess he could tell that I wasn't as into him as I used to be.

"Work, school, and Daijah. You know the drill." I tried to hide the sarcasm in my voice.

"What are you doing tonight? I could come over and bring a movie, and we can just hang out like old times."

"Not hanging with the boys?" I clearly had sarcasm in my voice this time.

"I'll rather hang with my baby."

"Well, not tonight, I have plans. As a matter of fact, I'm leaving in a minute."

"What do you mean? Where's Daijah?"

I rolled my eyes at his routine question. Daijah was always here, always with me, and always taken care of. I got the impression that he felt I shouldn't be going anywhere since I had her. Complete asshole, if you ask me.

"She's already asleep for the night and in bed with Mama. Hey, I'll call you tomorrow or when I get in, OK?"

"Wait, Cookie, what's going on? Are you going out with someone else?" Now, what if he knew that the person I was going out with was my first? Were Carlos and I exclusive anyway? I mean, what if the person only spends about an hour with you every now and then? Does that qualify to be "exclusive"? That routine was getting old.

"What do you mean am I going out with someone else?" I tried to hide the smile in my voice, but I couldn't help the fact that I enjoyed making Carlos feel threatened. He needed to know I wasn't at home, twirling my thumbs, waiting for him to show up whenever he could work me in his schedule.

"You heard my question, Cook. Don't play with me."

"Yeah, I heard, and yeah, I am going out with a group of folks," I lied. Now was not the time to display my soon-to-be cheating ways. I had been focused only on Carlos for so long that I was missing out on life.

"A group of folks, huh? You have never turned me down when I said I was coming over."

"Well, I know it'll only be about an hour you'll spend over here, and I want to have fun. So, no, thank you. I'll pass."

"What do you mean an hour? I spend more time over there than that."

"Oh yeah? When?" He grew quiet. "Look, Carlos, I got to go. I'll call you tomorrow."

"Tomorrow?"

"Yeah, tomorrow. I don't know when I'm getting back in."

He blew out air in frustration and hung up the phone without saying good-bye. *Oh really? He hung up on me. OK, I'll show him who's boss.* I slipped on my sandals, grabbed my purse, glanced in on Mama and Daijah, and walked out the front door. My date was awaiting me.

£££

Baron grinned from ear to ear as I walked toward him outside the movie theatre. "You look really good, Cookie."

I hugged him and told him thanks as he led the way to the lounge adjacent to the theatre. "We're going to eat here?"

"Yeah, I figured we could eat some burgers before the movie. That's cool with you?"

"Sure, I already know what I want," I said taking a seat at the nearest table.

I would be lying if I said I wasn't growing a brand-new crush on Baron. I always felt connected to him anyway because he was my first. I liked him so much I made sure to chew my food all the way through, and I left about a fourth of the food on my plate, not to seem greedy. Yeah, I was putting on an impression, loving the fact that someone was taking the time to be with me.

Cookie

The Day They Gave Me My Exit Papers

I bent down and looked at my daughter. Her eyes were lit up, and I could tell she was proud of me. She didn't know what was really going on, but the long blue gown and cap I wore gave me a wizard look, I guess. I leaned in and gave her a kiss and whispered that I loved her. Today I was going to be a high school graduate, and nothing was going to ruin my mood.

I turned and took Sierra's hand as we made our way into the auditorium. Then I glanced back, making sure Lyric was keeping an eye on Daijah like I had asked. Before I could pass the corner, I caught a glimpse of Mama sitting in her chair. She shot me a good luck wave, and I blew her a kiss. *Today I am making her a proud woman.*

My graduating class had over 250 kids, all anxious to get our diplomas and walk away, to never look back. I, for one, felt no different. I knew that the life I was living wasn't going to change once I was given a diploma.

I squeezed Sierra's hand one more time before we had to let go and take our assigned seats. I looked her in the eyes with tears forming and said, "This is it, Sierra. Today starts the rest of our lives."

"I know, girl. College, adult life, no obligations. I can't wait." I gave her a weak smile not trying to be jealous of her future, but who was I kidding? My future was being a mother and going to community college. And lots of obligations. This was it for me. Sierra gave me a reassuring smile and a hug before she walked away to take her seat.

I sat down in my seat and started to twirl my hair into my fingers to take away the nervousness. I was happy to be out of high school for sure, but for me, it was just another thing to do. I jumped up and looked toward the balcony when I heard someone scream my name and noticed my support system.

Surprising, Lola and Jayla were seated next to Mama, and I noticed Daijah in the arms of my daddy, who I hadn't seen since I gave birth to her. And then my eyes almost watered when I noticed Bishop in the audience, my old pastor from Higher Touch.

I stood up and as loud as I could yell, I said, "Hey, now, represent for me now." My classmates laughed when one of the teachers walked over to me and told me to have a seat. I thought about telling her to shut up because now I was grown. I could do whatever I wanted, but I decided to keep it cool tonight. Tonight was about me and no one else. I was graduating despite the odds of getting pregnant last year.

I turned my attention to the podium as the first speaker took the stand. I tuned out the speakers as soon as I felt my phone vibrate. I glanced at the phone and noticed a text from Carlos.

CARLOS: *I know we aren't in the best place, but I want to*
let you know that I'm proud of you. You did it.

I thought about texting back that I did it with little help from him. But what good would it do for me to hold a grudge against him? I was happy now. I was doing it mostly by myself, and I wasn't going to let anyone ruin my day. So I texted back.

COOKIE: *Thanks*

I scrolled through my numbers until I landed on Baron and shot him a text.

COOKIE: *Are you here?*

153

BARON: *Yeah, watching you play on your phone. Who
are you texting?*

COOKIE: *I'm texting you now. Thank you for these past
couple of weeks and being there for me.*

BARON: *Without a doubt, Cookie, I really should be
thanking you. We got a lifetime ahead of us,
and I can't wait for you to be a part of it.*

COOKIE: *Same here. I'll talk to you after the ceremony.*

It seemed as if time was on my side when I noticed they started to call out the names to come get their diploma. I glanced up and looked toward my family, my eyes stopping on Mama who was holding up her sign: *Congratulations, Cookie.*

I waved toward them and stood up when it was my row's turn. I took a quick glance back at Sierra and mouthed, "It's about that time." She clapped and cheered me on. I took my hand and wrapped it around the cold metal that led to the stairs of the stage. One by one, I moved closer to my principal who would hand me my key to adulthood.

I took my first step toward him as the announcer said, "Latoya James." I could have sworn my family was the most ghetto and loudest bunch in the whole stadium. I turned to look toward them when I saw the biggest red sign in the entire stadium.

"Ms. James, this way," I heard the principal say. I started to think over my life, the mistakes I made. The crowd Lyric had me hanging around, the money I stole, the bad checks I wrote, the clothes I stole, sneaking Carlos through my window, and now look at me. I got my diploma.

I walked toward the microphone without hesitation and saw the guard walking toward me to remove me so I hurriedly said, "Shout

out to all the haters who thought I wasn't going to amount to nothing. Watch me now." I blew a kiss into the air and turned toward the principal. "I'll take my diploma now." The crowd erupted into laughter and applause.

The principal leaned in and said, "Congratulations on graduating, Ms. James. You have a whole life ahead of you."

I smiled and said, "You have no idea."

Dear Mama

Two months after my graduation I was eighteen and saying good-bye to my best friend. She hopped on a flight headed to Washington, D.C. I envied the fact that she was going to go to a historic black college, but at the end of the day, we would both be successful. With Sierra's departure came in Baron's arrival. As if overnight, I took my heart and gave it to him. That was not my intention, but I guess it was easier to fall for him when you are alone.

I didn't take long to tell Carlos I was no longer going to wait on him. Life was short, and I refused to spend the rest of my days sitting at home waiting on him to show up whenever he felt like it. Plus, I promised Sierra I wouldn't do that, and, of course, I wouldn't let her down.

But Carlos suddenly had a change of heart and started becoming the active boyfriend and father I always wanted. Let's just say I was weighing my options now.

Today was like most days. I had started an internship at the Social Security office and had been making almost double of what I made at the restaurant waiting on tables. It was a little after four, and I had decided to go ahead and pick up Daijah and take her and Mama to Furr's Cafeteria.

Let me correct that. I thought today was going to be like most days, but today was different. Today marked the day of something I would never forget. Pulling up into the driveway, I parked and got Daijah out of the car. I had initially called home to tell Mama that I was going to take her out, but got no answer.

I opened the door and called out for Mama. I didn't hear her snores or the toxic smell of her gas in the air or the TV on. So I put Daijah down and told her to go watch TV in the living room. She ran off into the direction of the TV.

Walking down the hallway, I called Mama's name out again and heard nothing. I glanced in the bathroom to find it empty, and then turned the corner to her room. I stopped and thought, *Why in the world she is not answering me? She never sleeps this hard.*

Walking over to her in the bed, I stood over her and shook her on the shoulder. "Mama, wake up. I'm going to take you to Furr's." I waited a few seconds for her to respond. She didn't. I shook her shoulder again, and this is when I knew something was wrong.

"Mama!" I screamed. I could see in the corner of my eye Daijah standing behind me, not understanding what was wrong, but her face read that she knew something just wasn't right. I ran over to the other side of the bed and grabbed the phone.

Pressing 911, I leaned toward Mama to place my head on her chest. She was warm, but I couldn't feel or hear her breathing.

"What is your emergency?"

"My mother isn't breathing, I don't think. I can't wake her, and she isn't moving. I need an ambulance."

"I have your address and have sent an ambulance your way. They should be there within five minutes. Ma'am, can you tell me if your front door is unlocked?"

"Yes, it is."

"Is your mother on any medication?"

"Yes, she's on a lot of stuff."

"I need you to collect everything your mother takes and place it in a bag. I want you to bring it with you the hospital. Can you hear the sirens now, ma'am?"

"Yes, I can," I said as I placed Daijah on a bed and ran back into Mama's room, collecting bottles of pills that I saw. I heard a knock on the door. "They're here," I yelled into the phone. The operator assured me the paramedics can take it from there, and I raced to the door, dropping the phone in the process.

Opening the door I directed the paramedics to Mama. I looked back toward Daijah who was calling out to me. She was scared. I kept thinking, *I can not be losing my mama.*

Tamika Newhouse

Como Parade, 1996

It was the Fourth of July, and the summer heat was reaching about one hundred and two degrees. I had on my new khaki shorts and my shirt that read, *Do the Tootsies Roll?* I ran over to my Big Mama who was seated in her lounge chair on the edge of the street and asked for another piece of the candy she was throwing.

She smiled down at me and said, "Anything for my baby." I was the youngest out of all my seventy-odd cousins, and it was pretty safe to say that I got away with mostly everything.

I ran over and stood next to Lyric, Jayla, Lynn, and some of my other cousins who had their bags ready to catch the candy the people on the floats were throwing our way. I turned back when I heard someone call my name. "Cookie, make sure you get a lot of candy." I smiled toward my Aunt Flo, who was seated next to my other aunts, and waved. I just knew I was going to get the most candy.

Today was the annual Fourth of July parade hosted in Como every year. Como was the oldest black neighborhood in Fort Worth. It was pretty poor and housed some of the oldest real estate, but it was our neighborhood. Like our own little city.

I glanced up and saw a float hosting Viola Pitts. I didn't know who she was then but would soon discover she was an activist for Como for years, making sure this community of ours got funding from the city and better schools. I waved toward her, and she threw candy toward me and my cousins. We took to the ground picking up all the pieces that we could get.

Excited about the big pile of candy and gum I accumulated, I ran up to Mama, who was seated by Lola, and said, "Look, Mama, I got all of this candy."

"You do, girl. You're going to have to share some of that with me," she laughed.

"Nope." I hid the bag behind my back and started to laugh.

She lifted me up and sat me in her lap, reaching down to grab the wine cooler she was drinking. I stared at it and said, "Mama, let me taste it."

"Cookie, when you get grown, pay your own bills, and take care of me, perhaps I'll let you taste my wine cooler."

"Cookie, why don't you go play with the kids?" Lola said, pointing toward my cousins.

"It's hot," I whined. I leaned back onto Mama's chest and listened to her laugh about a woman's outfit that was way too tight for her size. I loved to lie on her chest and listen to her voice from the inside. It sounded about the same, but I felt like no one else could hear it but me; like I was getting an exclusive listen to her soul.

She turned her head to yell toward one of my uncles to get her another wine cooler and me a bottle of water. I had to wipe away her Jheri curl juice that had found its way brushing across my forehead.

My whole family was out here today on our block on Fletcher Street. Even Big Mama had left her porch to join us on the corner to enjoy the parade. Her house stood just across the street, the same house most of my twelve aunts and uncles grew up in from the fifties.

I looked up toward Mama and examined her chocolate skin. It was almost as black as her hair, but had a smooth texture to it. The men who used to court her called her "Blackberry," whatever that meant.

In all of my life I had never seen Mama with a man. As I grew up, I learned that she hid men from us to make sure her girls were always protected. I always thanked her for that.

I was happy to see her because since she worked two jobs, and Lola was pretty much my active parent, I rarely saw her. We lived in the same house, but Mama had a night and day job, and a week could pass and I wouldn't catch a sight of her. So when I saw her, I clung to her like a baby.

We didn't hug much or kiss, but I didn't need that to know that she loved me. She showed it in her actions, like now. I was snuggled under her bosom like it wasn't as hot as it was and over a hundred degrees, and she hadn't told me to move yet.

She looked toward me and said, "Cookie, you feeling hot."

"No, Mama, I'm OK."

She kissed my forehead, a rare occurrence, and said, "You going to grow up to be as pretty as your mama."

I smiled and nodded my head. "I wanna have your skin too, Mama. It's so dark and smooth."

"You may be brown now, but I can see it. You are going to be black as hell, just like your mama." She squeezed me tightly.

"So I can have a wine cooler if I take care of you when I grow up?"

She laughed and said, "Cookie, you can have just about anything in this world when you grow up. And guess what?"

"What?" I asked.

"I'm going to be right beside you cheering you on." I wrapped my arms around her neck and gave her a tight squeeze before jumping off her lap to join my cousins. I turned back around and looked toward

162

her again. She waved and told me to go play and have fun. Thinking back now, I did have fun. I had the time of my life that day.

£££

My thoughts were interrupted from that day when I noticed I was standing still at a green light; the ambulance Mama was in was long gone, but I knew where they were going. I didn't hesitate to call Lyric to tell her to meet us at the hospital, and as I pulled into the parking lot of the Plaza Medical Center, my phone rang.

I looked at the caller ID and saw my Aunt Flo's number. "Hey, Aunt Flo."

"Lyric just called me. Della is in the hospital?"

"Yes, I just pulled up now. I came home, and she wouldn't wake up."

"I'm on my way up there with Kita." Kita was my other aunt. I told her I'd see her then and pulled Daijah out of her car seat and made my way through the emergency doors. Making my way to the nurses' station, I asked for where they had Della James.

I was told that until she was stabilized that I had to wait. I gripped my daughter's hand and the bag of pills and took a seat by the front door. I don't know why I chose to sit so far away. Maybe I felt like if I needed to escape I could do so by running through those doors. But it wouldn't hide the fact that I was seated here waiting to know whether or not my mother was OK.

Daijah brought her tiny hand to my face and moved it to where I faced her. She looked at me with so much concern. I couldn't have her worrying about me. I gave her a fake smile and said, "It's OK. You want something from the machine over there?"

She nodded her head yes as I pulled quarters out of my purse and walked us over to the machine. I selected animal crackers for her and pulled open the bag so that she could eat it. As I turned around I heard Lyric's voice. She had Renzel with her.

"What happened?" She was crying. I could tell she had been. Then I wondered why I hadn't cried yet. I was nervous and my heart felt like it was going to burst out of my chest, but I hadn't cried.

"I don't know yet. They're stabilizing her." Together we sat down and waited for an answer from the doctor or someone to come and see us. Fifteen minutes passed when a black male in a white coat ask for the James family.

As I stood up, I felt as if someone else were standing on my feet as I forced myself to take each step toward him. Lyric grabbed my hand, and I flinched, not used to her showing genuine emotion toward me.

Lyric said, "That's us!"

Tamika Newhouse

Cookie

Val Verde Drive, 1999

I had my knees clutched to my chest. I tried to knock out the screams and the yelling, but it wasn't working. I figured if I hid in my closet, I wouldn't have to witness Lyric run away from home. I didn't care if she stayed or not, but Mama surely did, which meant I had to also.

When coming home from school I sensed something wasn't right. The bus driver was nice enough to drop me off in front of the house, but when I stepped off and noticed a black duffle bag and a few clothes sprawled across the ground, I knew something was wrong.

I heard Lyric's voice scream out that she was leaving. I ran up to the front door, and like the other fights Mama had with Lyric, I saw her pen Lyric up against the wall with her fist buried into Lyric's chest. *What happened now?*

Mama screamed, "You think you grown now and can have sex? Look at your fast tail. You done gone and got Chlamydia."

What's Chlamydia? I didn't know then but would soon find out that the guy Mama swore up and down that Lyric was dating was mentally unstable and had given Lyric an STD. I remembered a couple days ago Lyric complaining about having a pain when she peed. Apparently we all knew why now.

Not the one to butt into any argument they ever had, I dodged behind them and ran down the hallway to my room. For a minute there I thought about calling Lola and telling her what Lyric had done. As if the fighting and getting suspended from school and having sex with

166

random boys wasn't enough, now she wanted to run away from home. *Good riddance.*

I hated Lyric more and more each day when she came home with some new drama. But Mama wouldn't let Lyric go for nothing. She fought with her and warned her many times. But Lyric's agenda was always her current boyfriend.

When I heard the front door open and the sound from the glass bursting, I ran out and saw Lyric trying to pick up her clothes.

"You think you grown now, huh?" Mama screamed out. She reached over toward Lyric and pushed her up against the brick wall. *Man, she likes to hem us up against the wall.* I, however, hadn't had the pleasure of Mama throwing me up against the wall yet; I saw how it hurt Lyric so much that I didn't dare do anything to have Mama do it to me. When I saw the anger in Lyric's eyes, I ran out, afraid she would try to hit back. One thing we always knew was no matter how many times our mama whooped us, we *never* swung back.

I reached in toward Mama and Lyric and tried to squeeze in between them. But my small frame wasn't making much of an impact.

I yelled out, "Y'all stop!"

I felt like my rib cage was squeezed around my lungs as I tried to make some type of impact on separating them. They both were big women in my opinion, with Lyric about fifty pounds heavier than me, and Mama just plain big. I couldn't do much but attempt to separate them and yell at the same time. When they were both out of breath they backed up. Huffing and puffing, we all stared at each other as our white neighbors were now peeking out of their windows wondering if they should call the cops.

"You grown. Get your stuff and leave. But if you leave, don't come back," Mama said, walking off, her steps leading her back into our home. I bet if Lyric looked back on this day now, she would be ashamed, knowing that in the future, the same guy she wanted to run away and be with would soon commit murder and be sentenced to prison for life.

Lyric didn't leave that day. She picked up all her clothes and made it all the way to the end of the street. Guess she realized that at the end of the day, she had nowhere else to go but here with us.

£££

I had made it into the Critical Care Unit with Lyric and walked into Room B. That was Mama's room. It was a lot colder in here than it was in the lobby, so I was glad Daijah was in the lobby with Renzel.

Reluctantly, I took Lyric's hand, and we walked in together. *Your mother's diabetes has taken a turn for the worse, and her kidneys have failed. We had to place a tube down her throat to help her breathe.* The doctor's voice played over and over in my head as I took a step into Mama's room.

You could hear the sound of the breathing machine pumping air into my mother's body. She lay still. Only her chest moved up and down.

I took my free hand and wiped away the tears that found their way to the surface. *Wonder what we got to do this time for her to come home.* This wasn't Mama's first trip to the hospital. Maybe the tenth in two years.

"She don't look so good," Lyric said.

168

I nodded that I agreed but was afraid to say it out loud. I wrapped my hands around Mama's feet. They were cold. I started to massage them to get some warmth back into them, and then covered them back up with her bedsheet.

Not much was said between Lyric and me as we both made sure Mama was comfortable, placing footies onto her feet and throwing an extra blanket around her body. The nurse walked in behind us and said, "Ladies, you have some family outside."

We eyed each other as I said, "Let's go see who it is." I looked back toward the nurse and said, "Don't let anyone else in yet." The nurse nodded as we made our way back down the hallway.

I reached for the double doors and pushed them open. My mouth dropped when I saw the many people in the hallway. "What in the world!"

I eyed Lyric, who was just as shocked as I was. At least fifty folks stood in the hallway leading the Critical Care Unit, most I knew. Cousins, aunts, uncles, and Mama's old friends gathered.

"How in the world did you all get here so fast?"

Aunt Flo walked up to me and said, "How is she?" She was clearly trying to make her way back to the unit. I glanced over her shoulder before I could reply and saw security walking toward me.

"I'm sorry, but we can't have all of these people near the front doors. We are going to have to ask you all to wait in the waiting room," the security guard called out.

I nodded that I understood and yelled out to the family to go up front. I didn't need to be reminded that my family was the most unruly, loudest bunch I had ever seen. Aunt Flo repeated her question while I noticed my Aunt Kita and Debra walk up to me.

"She was placed on a breathing machine. The doctor hasn't told us anything new yet but said he would within the hour."

"I called Howard," Aunt Debra called out. I gave her that why-the-hell-did-you-do-that look. *Maybe he's out of town driving his truck.* "He'll be here in a bit." I wanted to curse under my breath.

With everyone following one another, it looked like a civil rights movement march. I turned the corner and noticed my grandparents. I walked over to them and gave them a bear hug. With Big Mama in the nursing home, Mama's only parents to be here were Papa and his wife.

"How's Della?" my papa asked. I nodded my head and said that we were waiting on the doctor, but it didn't look good. I found Daijah sitting in Renzel's lap. She whined that she was hungry.

I flipped open my phone and dialed the only person I knew she would want right now. "Hey, Carlos, I need you right now." I didn't waste any time getting to the point.

It sounded like he was busy, but I didn't care. I needed him at this moment. He replied, "Cook, what's wrong? You don't sound good."

"I need you to meet me at the Plaza Medical Center on 8th Avenue."

"Why are you at the hospital?"

"It's Mama; it's bad. And I can't watch Daijah right now."

"Oh, man, I'm on my way." I heard him getting up.

"Can you bring Daijah some food too?" I hung up the phone and dialed Lola.

"I'm on the highway now," she said. "How is she?" I looked up and saw the doctor who came and got me and Lyric before.

He called out, "The James family." I could have sworn he said James but at least thirty folks stood up to ambush the doctor. Security came immediately to break us up. *Will they sit their butt down and let me and Lyric handle this?* I was too embarrassed at the scene my family was creating.

"I'm sorry. I just need her daughters," the doctor said. My cousin Reann didn't take too kindly to the doctor shooing them away as she still proceeded to make her way toward him.

"How's my aunt? Is she OK?" I understood Reann being worried since she was my mama's favorite niece, but I was agitated at the fact my mama was dying and I couldn't talk to her doctor in peace.

I turned toward my family. All of them looked worn out and miserable. Some had been crying; some were sleepy because it was late. Regardless of these facts, it was a no-win situation to get them to act civil. "We'll be right back." I grabbed Lyric's hand who was quiet and not much of any help keeping our family in check and followed the doctor down the long hallway leading to the Critical Care Unit.

We stopped midway when he turned to us and said, "Who is Ms. James's power of attorney?"

Remembering the medical papers Mama had me and Lola sign a few months back, I said, "I am. Why?"

"Do you know of your mother's wishes?" *OK, these questions don't sound too good. If this Negro don't tell me what's up, I'm going to slap him with his own medical board.*

"Doctor … Todd, is it. Yes, Doctor Todd, can you tell me why you're asking us this?" Lyric said.

"Your mother has been incubated, and her heart has weakened. When a patient like Ms. James is placed on a breathing

171

machine, they are more likely to crash within the first twenty-four hours."

Comprehending I said, "As in flat line?" Remembering the medical talk on the show *ER*, I started to replay scenes in my head when the doctors tried to revive their patients.

"Yes ma'am. She will more likely flat line, and we need to know your mother's wishes. Her kidneys have now failed, and we are placing her on dialysis."

"Can we put her on a transplant list?" I asked.

He shook his head no and said, "With the level of your mother's sickness, her weight, and her diabetes, she will not be a great candidate." *Is he telling me that my mother won't be able to have new kidneys? What does this mean?*

Not taking my eyes off the doctor, I said, "Doctor Todd, what are you saying?"

"It's not good; if we try to revive her, she will more likely not wake up. She will need to stay on dialysis for the remainder of her life. We need to know if it is your mother's wishes to use heroic measures."

"You mean she ain't waking up?" Lyric repeated.

"Is she brain-dead, Doc?"

"She has very little brain activity, Ms. James. I'm sorry."

I stared at him for a moment, hoping that my looks could kill him. I couldn't believe he was standing here telling me that this was the moment, the moment I knew was coming for a while now. But no matter what I felt, I already knew the answer. I took my feelings away and thought about Mama. Of course she wouldn't want to be bedridden; she didn't want to be brain dead or paralyzed; and she didn't want this for her life.

I knew what I had to say, but at this moment, my heart started to burn, as if it was beating irregular. I breathed in deeply and exhaled, taking my time to answer him. It was up to me. Mama made me her power of attorney, meaning I had complete control of her life. What I said would determine if I allowed her soul to rest.

But surprisingly, it was easy; I loved my mother more than life itself, but to have her suffer because I wanted her here was out of the question. I wanted *her* here not her body. And if she wasn't going to wake up, that wasn't useful for me, Lyric, or Daijah.

Oh my Lord, I forgot about Daijah. What am I going to tell her what happened to her big granny? Would she even understand?

I turned my attention to Lyric whose eyes were bloodshot. She looked horrified. I guess the thought of Mama being gone was starting to sink in. I looked at her and placed my hands on both of her shoulders. "Lyric, this is it. Are you ready?"

Her body started to sink and give out as she cried out, "No!"

"This is it, Lyric. Are you ready?" I asked again through my own sobs. I couldn't even recognize my own voice as I spoke. My mouth was dry, and my eyes burned from the tears that felt like hot steam coming out of them. "This is it," I said one more time.

I knew this was it, the moment I never wanted to come. My mama wasn't going to be here anymore. I wasn't going to hear her laugh anymore, hear her slam the dominoes on the table when she made a great play. I wasn't going to be consumed with the toxic smell of her gas anymore. I wouldn't witness her shouting out in church in approval of the pastor's sermon, I wouldn't watch a basketball game with her anymore. I wouldn't even hear her voice. I knew this was it.

Looking at Doctor Todd I said, "I want a DNR, sir."

173

He flipped some pages on his clipboard and asked me if I was certain. I knew I was. No way would I have my mother suffer a horrible, long death. I nodded my head yes and took his ballpoint pen in my hand. I glanced toward Lyric who had mouthed the words OK, as I placed the pen on the paper to sign.

My hand almost shook uncontrollably as I signed Latoya James. "We will keep her comfortable," the doctor said as he walked off in the direction of my mother's room.

Grabbing Lyric's hand I asked her if she was ready. We knew our family was waiting for us to return. She solemnly nodded her head yes as we walked back down the long white hallway leading to the waiting room.

Aunt Kita ran toward me. "What did he say, Cookie?" I took a deep breath as one by one my family gathered around us. Lyric stood behind me, I guess to hide and take cover. A storm was brewing.

I started off repeating what the doctor said and finally got the courage to say I had signed a DNR.

"You *what?*" Aunt Flo yelled.

"It's what she would have wanted."

Cousin Reann leaned in toward me and screamed, "How the hell could you let her die? That's my aunt in there, and you going to kill her?"

My frustration, anger, and fear kicked into high gear when I pointed my finger in her face and said, "Bitch, how the hell you going to come in my face and say some mess like that?" I charged my body toward her but felt interference when I was held back by Renzel and Lyric.

One of my other aunts who I hadn't seen in years yelled out, "Della would want to live!" *How the hell do you know? You ain't been around in over five years.* It dawned on me that everyone had something to say now, but no one was there to help me when Mama was sick and couldn't move around her house. I did it all alone. No one had anything to say then, but when it came down to her last wishes, they all had plenty to say. That was some bull if you ask me.

Security pulled me back into an empty patient room where Daijah was sound asleep. I was boiling over in anger. Then I heard security on the other side of the door threatening to kick everyone out. *Why does my family have to act ghetto when my mama is down the hall dying?*

£££

Thirty minutes had passed, and Lyric and I were seated in the waiting room with the family after someone went and bought some William's Chicken. I took a bite and sat next to Aunt Debra, the one who was most understanding.

"How you doing, Cookie?" she asked.

"It's not easy. I'm holding it together though."

"I think you're doing good taking control over all of this. Now that's my sister in there, and I love her, but you know her best. You know what she wants."

I nodded my head and took a bite from my chicken when the overhead speaker came on. Code Blue in CCU Room B. Cold Blue in CCU Room B.

Wait a minute! That's Mama's room, right?

I threw my food down and took off. I couldn't feel my feet hitting the floor as I rushed to make my way down the hallway.

175

Nothing mattered to me at this moment but finding out if it was my mother who was dying. When I pushed open the doors that led to her unit I felt a brush behind me and turned. It was Lyric. She had run after me.

She walked past me as I was unable to walk any further. I kept repeating, "Is it her room? Is it her?" Lyric walked in and stopped in front of Mama's room. Her face said nothing, and her eyes were empty. It was if her life left her at this moment.

"Is it her?" I screamed.

She turned toward me. Her eyes filled with tears, and her bottom lip spread thin and quivering. "It's her. It's her, Cookie."

I started to scream even before I knew I was screaming as my legs gave out on me and I fell to the ground. My dress flew up in the air as I repeated over and over, "No, not my mama." The realization of letting her go and signing that DNR was more real than it ever was before. My mother was no more. She was no longer here. I do remember that I signed those papers in order for her to rest in peace. It wasn't about me. It was time to let her pain end. I fell out on the floor and screamed until my voice gave out. And even then, I didn't stop screaming, hoping that her spirit heard my cries and changed her mind about leaving me. But it didn't work.

Tamika Newhouse

This Too Will Be a Faded Memory

I rolled over to the other side of the bed and stretched my arms. I immediately felt a massive headache from being up so late the night before. I raised my head and looked toward my bedroom door. It was quiet.

Placing my foot over the side of the bed, I twirled my toes into the carpet, rubbing my eyes in the process. I looked toward the clock on my bedside table. It read eight o'clock. I was glad Daijah was with Carlos. I didn't feel up to fixing her breakfast.

I got up and walked toward the door, stopping just before I walked out as I noticed Mama's room across the hallway. The TV wasn't on. I couldn't hear her snoring. And I didn't smell the odor of food cooking. She wasn't here. We buried her a week ago.

I rushed past her door and the bathroom door, walking into the living room. Until this very moment I loved this house. It was where I called home since I was three. Many people lived here from cousins, uncles, aunts, Lola, and Jayla. Now, everyone was gone, including Mama.

I rushed toward the house phone and dialed. He picked up on the first ring. "Are you OK?"

"Baron, I need to move out of this house. I can't take it any longer." I was crying. The tightness in my voice led to me to believe I was crying harder than I thought.

"OK, babe, calm down. Where's Daijah?"

"With her daddy, and it's so quiet. I can't take it anymore. I got to get out of here." I was yelling at this point.

178

"OK, I want you to grab a bag of clothes and some things for Daijah, and I want you to come over here."

"You want me to come there?"

"Yes, do it now while you're on the phone so I know you're all right."

I wiped the snot from my nose and did what I was told. Passing the wall that held the inches of Daijah's height from her first year of birth, passing the hole in the wall that came from a fight during a party back in '92, passing the sign on the wall that I created in middle school that said, *Everyone wants to go to heaven but no one wants to go to church*, I passed the photos of Lynn, Lyric, Jayla, and I that were posted on the wall, I overlooked the nightstand Mama loved so much and had in layaway for over six months, I chose not to look at Mama's Bible that was still laying on the table where she had left it. I just walked toward my room. The room I have lived in most of my life. I grabbed a duffle bag and threw some tennis shoes, shirts, and shorts in. Then I did the same with Daijah's clothes. Finished, I ran back toward the living room and grabbed Mama's car keys. I pulled opened the door, allowing the fall weather to brush across my skin, and locked the door behind me.

This was the only home I knew, but today, it was the reminder of how much things had changed. Nothing was the same. Not even I could overlook that.

£££

I felt him trail his hands over my back, giving it a tight squeeze as he brought me closer into his embrace. He smelled good this early in the morning. I was glad it was a Saturday and he was home and

179

not at work. We collapsed on his bed together, and I buried my face in his neck, taking in the smell of soap from his recent shower.

Baron said, "You know, Cook, we have been through some things together. From the shoot-out in Gateway Park, to us making love, to the night I got shot, to you having Daijah, and now this. Baby, I know you feel like life is pretty messed up right now, but I love you and no matter what, we are going to get through this too."

I looked at him, trying to see if he was bluffing, but he looked so sincere. I leaned in and kissed his lips. "I love you too, Baron." And I did. He was my first; he had saved my life on more than one occasion. Why wouldn't I love him?

For once I didn't think about Mama dying or my family disowning me because I didn't do what they wanted me to do. I blocked out the conversation I had with Aunt Flo who called and screamed in my ear, blaming everything on me.

I would be lying if I said I wasn't hurt by her words or my family's disapproval, but I knew that at the end of the day, I did what was best for my mama and not them. I had to remind myself that.

Baron got up and said, "Are you hungry? I can make you something to eat."

I sucked in my bottom lip, rubbing my tongue across it, and said, "Baron, the only thing I want to do is feel you in my arms right now." I extended my arms, allowing him to lie in my bosom. I spread my legs and arched my back and whispered, "I want to feel *you* too."

He smiled, leaned down, and pressed power on his radio. R. Kelly's voice started to croon through the air. For if only one moment I allowed myself to relax and pretend that my whole world wasn't crashing in.

Tamika Newhouse

Take Me As I Am

I wanted to drive Baron's truck. Finally he gave in and let me drive it. I loved the power I felt when driving that big rig. I had finally gotten back to work, and it was going on three weeks since the funeral. Carlos was nice enough in my opinion to let Daijah stay with him and his mother till I got things settled. I ended up settling at Baron's apartment. We had a blended family going on with Baron and his son, and Daijah loved both of them. Funny thing is, I hadn't told Carlos yet.

I'll probably tell him when I felt like it. After picking up the order I placed for us at Pizza Hut, I felt my phone buzz. I flipped it open and said, "Hello."

"Well, well, well, I see you have come from under Baron and his fine ass."

"Sierra, here you go. Found time to call and check on me, huh?" She laughed and I had to pull the phone away from my ear.

"Girl, classes here ain't no joke. I should have just stayed there with you."

"Girl, for what? Ain't anything going on in Funkytown. Just same ole folks doing nothing. I wanna be like you when I grow up," I mocked.

"You doing good though? Did you get everything moved out of Mama's house?"

"Just about. Lola is putting it up for sale. It should go quick."

"What's that music in the background? Don't tell me you listening to gospel." She laughed again. I was riding past Morning Side

182

Baptist and like most Baptist churches, you could always hear their music from the street.

"Girl, no. I'm just passing by one on the street." I looked up at the stoplight and saw that it had turned green. Just when I was ready to pull off, a familiar tune started to play.

Pass me not, O gentle Savior

Hear my humble cry

While on others thou art calling

Do not pass me by

Savior, Savior

Hear my humble cry

I immediately started to sing the familiar Baptist hymn. "Sierra, let me call you back." I didn't wait for her to reply. I clicked the phone shut, turning the truck to the direction of the church. The parking lot was full of cars so I parked on the side of the road and hopped out. The music was still playing as I felt myself getting emotional. I hadn't attended church much since I had entered high school back in 2000. Mama had stopped making us go.

I immediately tried to pull down my skirt as I placed my hand on the front door and walked in. My thoughts were interrupted when I heard a screechy voice say, "Can I help you?"

"Oh, no, thank you. I'm just going to sit in the back."

She raised her hand toward my chest halting my steps.

What the hell is her problem?

"We are a sophisticated bunch, and we do not allow strays into the church dressed like, well, like you," she snarled at me. She was clearly taking her job as an usher too far.

I looked down over my outfit and brushed my hands over my blouse that barely covered my navel and pulled at my short skirt. OK, she wasn't lying. It was a little ho-ish, but damn, I ain't never been blackballed at a church before.

"Ma'am, I just really need to get in there. I feel like I'm supposed to be here." The words to the song continued to play, and I yearned to go inside and allow the music to sing to my soul. I was hurting. I wanted to let it out, regardless of the fact that I was a sinner now, far away from the Christian I used to be.

"I'm sorry. You're going to have to change if you want to be let into the sanctuary."

I felt like I was being denied access to a club. I noticed a choir robe hanging on a coatrack behind her. I rushed past her, pulled it down, and wrapped it around my shoulders. Being as tall as I was, it barely covered my calves.

"There, are you happy now?" I wanted to say, *you angry bitch.* I repented for having the thoughts in my head while on church grounds.

She looked down and smirked, planting her eyes on my black heels. "You can't go in with those on your feet."

You've got to be kidding me. I was one second off from whooping this old woman's ass. Who the hell was she to deny me access to the church because I wasn't dressed like an old maid?

"Now you're trippin' on my shoes?"

"Watch your tone, young lady." She wagged her boney finger in my face, and I gave her my most disgusted look. She was evil as hell, and I was one second away from letting her know just that.

"Watch *my* tone? Look at you trying to control who comes in the church. This is supposed to be a place of refuge, you evil—" I

184

stopped in midsentence and thought the song was almost over. I am not going to miss this. I reached down and unhooked the strap on my shoes and kicked them toward her. I was hoping that they somehow hit her but not really.

"Look, see now; you can't complain," I said with an attitude.

"You have any more shoes?" she snarled at me. I rolled my eyes and pushed her out of my way. I heard her calling after me, but I didn't pay her no mind. The song was almost over. I needed to get inside.

I pushed open the sanctuary doors and the congregation was in a trance. Everyone's hands were raised, and eyes were closed. They were calling out on the name of the Lord. I immediately felt a rush as my eyes became misty. I opened my mouth and recited the lyrics, hoping that somehow with each phrase I spoke it took away the heavy burden of my heart.

Walking straight down the aisle I could still hear that annoying usher calling for me to come back. I was going to complain about her later. I closed my eyes as I continued to walk, hoping that the Spirit led me straight to the altar.

My mind quickly started to recount my life, my absent father, my toxic relationship with my sister, the death of Trent, the rape of Sierra, my church disbanding, being attacked and having Baron almost die, becoming pregnant, breaking things off with Carlos, and now this. The only person I truly loved was gone. I opened my mouth and screamed out, "I need someone to pray for me." Then I cried.

I could barely see over the tears that were clouding my eyes. My mouth was dry. I didn't bother to wipe the saliva that had formed. I fell to the ground mere steps away from the altar. The pastor looked down and called out, "Come on to the house of the Lord. That's it. Come on."

The rough wool from the carpet felt like it was cutting into my knees, but I continued to crawl, hoping that it got me closer to the altar. I slid my legs back and forth and used my hands to feel for the first steps. *I feel it.* I fell forward, throwing my body onto the steps. I felt a hand go over the back of my head and realized it was the pastor. I cried out in agony, praying for God to help me. To help me heal as my mind went to a place that was all too familiar.

Tamika Newhouse

Higher Touch Fellowship Church 1997

I stood next to Jayla and Lyric as we clapped to the song Bishop was playing. I looked across the room and noticed Carlos wink. I smiled back and went back to enjoying the latest gospel song. Lola came up and took the microphone, yelling into the air saying, "I can't hear you, saints. J-E-S-U-S."

I bopped my head to the beat and looked back toward Mama, who was jumping up and down waving her handkerchief. "Hey, now!" she yelled out in acceptance. I laughed and turned back toward the stage.

Everyone was on their feet dancing to the music. Chairs had been moved away, and people were shouting. I turned to Lyric and said, "Do this," clapping in a rhythm and stomping my feet. She followed suit.

Jayla noticed our new dance step and joined in, creating a small dance group. I looked up and noticed Lynn walk over and join in. We had a gospel soul train going on.

I threw my head back and enjoyed the excitement of the service. My smile spread wide across my face. I heard Bishop call out, "Cookie, Lyric, hey, y'all, come up front and show the saints how the youth get down. Come on," he said over his microphone.

Lyric laughed and pulled my hand. Lynn and Jayla followed. We walked in the very front of the church and stood in a straight line. Then I started the clap again, motioning for everyone to follow. We stomped our feet and clapped our hands as the congregation cheered us on. I looked over my church family seeing all of them smile, shout out in praise, and join in our step.

I looked back toward our section where Mama was. I could see her white handkerchief swaying in the air. I laughed, thinking she's the funniest person up in here. She ran up and said, "Let me in this, Bishop." She squeezed in between Lyric and me, and the crowd yelled out, "Go on, Sister Della."

She placed her hands on her hips and jumped from side to side, pushing her big hip into mine. I laughed in embarrassed excitement. Looking up, I saw Carlos laugh. I smiled toward him and put some more motion into my step.

"Go on, Mama," Lyric yelled out.

Mama grabbed my hand, and we did a two-step dance together, showing the congregation that back in the day she could really move.

I squeezed her hand and yelled out, "You are funny, Mama."

She looked down toward me and said, "Girl, move them feet. Let the devil know he won't win." I took my feet and stomped harder on the ground, imagining the devil's head underneath my feet. *Yeah, that'll show the devil. I am not the one to mess with. I'm going to make it in this world. If the Lord says the same, just like my mama, I'm going to make it.*

ONE YEAR LATER

The End Of The Beginning

I laughed out as Daijah tried to tell me how her day was in pre-k. I didn't know who or what she was talking about, but it was so interesting to her. "OK, Ms. Igotastorytotell, go hang up your backpack, will you?"

I walked into the kitchen of my apartment and found Baron sitting at the table with his son, trying to fix him a snack. I reached in behind him and hugged him, kissing him on the back of his neck.

"Well, well, well, how is my baby doing today?"

"Just fine. Class today wasn't all that bad. My professor didn't talk me to death, and then work, well, you know how that is," I said, pulling a bottle of water out of the refrigerator. Then I walked over to Baron Jr. and gave him a kiss.

Baron said, "Hey, do you think Carlos can watch Daijah this weekend? I got my mother watching Junior because I want to take you somewhere special. It's your birthday, you know."

"Yeah, I know. I'm leaving my teen years. Ugh, I'm going to be getting old after awhile," I joked.

"Don't go there," he said, playfully throwing a dish towel my way.

I walked out of the kitchen into our bedroom, picked up the phone receiver, and dialed Carlos.

"Hey, beautiful, what's up?"

190

Rolling my eyes at his constant reminder that he still wanted to be together I said, "You know it's my birthday coming up, right?"

"Yep, sure do. So where do you want me to take you?" he joked.

"Ha-ha, Carlos. I wanted to know if Daijah can come over tonight. I'm going out with Lynn, Lyric, and Kyra," I lied.

"Oh, so a girls' night out. You mean Mr. Perfect ain't taking my baby out?"

"Ugh. Carlos, can she come or not?"

"You know my baby can come see her daddy whenever."

"Thank you. I'll call you back. My other line is beeping." I clicked over before he could say anything else and said, "Hello."

"Hi, this is Doctor Jones at Harris Methodist. Is Latoya James available?"

Harris Hospital? Now what?

"This is she. Why?"

"Ma'am, we need to know if you are able to come to the hospital; it's about your sister."

"My sister?"

"Yes, Lyric James has been in an accident."

My heart dropped. It had only been a couple months since she was let out of prison for fraud charges. I hadn't had the chance to really spend time with her, being busy with school and work.

"What kind of accident, sir?" I swallowed hard, afraid of what he might say.

"I can't discuss much over the phone, but her boyfriend gave me this number. She was hit by a car."

"Hit by a car?"

191

"Yes. A few times. Can you come to the ICU as soon as possible? We need her next of kin."

I dropped the phone as my mind started to race. I thought everything was finally good. I thought that the worst was over. I thought everything was going to be OK. Maybe I was wrong. I could hear the doctor's voice calling my name, wanting to know if I was still there.

I wasn't there. I wasn't anywhere. My mind was stuck on the fact that again I was in this dark place.

Not again!

Coming from Delphine Publications in 2012

69 Degres By Felisha Bradshaw

Who Do I Run To? By Anna Black

Hotel 23 By Norris E. Pimpton Jr.

Find classic novels from Delphine Publications at
www.delphinepublications.com